At the crack of the rifle, she cringed while his right shoulder exploded with blood, flesh, and bone spurting everywhere. He dropped in full flight.

With her mind reeling, she raced back to the safety of some trees. Gasping for breath, she chanced a peak and saw Danny lying still. This couldn't be happening.

The shooter skirted past him at a dead run. Beth had to hide. She had to get to the thick covering of the trees near the large magnetic anomaly.

The shooter glanced at the blood stained body on the ground. Without slowing, he headed in Beth's direction. Even when he lost sight of her, he checked places she had only gone to when alone. Without a doubt, Shorty's days of spying had paid off.

Beth hid quietly under a tree's large branches. As each second ticked by, she heard the birds and the monkeys get louder and louder. She breathed deeply to calm her shivering body. Who the hell had shot the gun? There was no rhyme or reason for it. The sounds around her stilled and she sensed he was close. Cold steel touched her shoulder as the barrel of the .223 caliber rifle found its mark. She stiffened as a wave of nausea threatened to bring up her lunch.

"Get up!" commanded the voice. "Thought you could hide, huh? I know you better than you know yourself."

Recognizing the voice, she understood why he needed her alive. Slowly, she got to her feet.

Betrayal In Paradise

Champagne Books Presents

Betrayal in Paradise

By

Danny Hangartner

To Steve,
Thank you for
everything. Your
friend,
[signature]

Champagne Books
www.champagnebooks.com
Copyright © 2006 by Daniel Hangartner
ISBN 1897261829
February 2007
Cover Art © Chris Butts
Produced in Canada

Champagne Books
#35069-4604 37 ST SW
Calgary, AB T3E 7C7
Canada

Dedication

My brother's first wife helped me sort out my first novel,
and gave me a direction in my writing. Helen rests in peace.

One

Shrill winds bent huge, white poplars over concrete sidewalks and paved streets. Sashaying leaves danced with flying paper, harmonizing with large rolling tumbleweeds. Specks of salt and dust peppered endless streams of speeding mud-caked vehicles traveling over the dirty, frost-heaved roads. Turbulent eddies dramatized an early sunny spring day in Slave Lake, Alberta. Judging order in the wind's responsibility to move spring into summer, Danny believed an orderly undertaking in his life was something to consider. Wondering what to do, he walked around as he tried to sort things out.

Gusts of dirt resonated off a travel agency's large windowpane, pitching now the time is ripe to travel. Be somewhere else!

Hesitating, he turned toward the inviting sounds. In his reflection, he thought about others arriving as the season turned into summer. Caring less, he needed his own change for the better. Flustered by the stinging winds, his watery eyes squinted through the window's mirrored sunlight. Piercing green eyes sought the shade of their own reflection before finding the inside of the small, northern town's solitary travel agency.

A blonde-haired travel agent sat posture perfect in front of a computer at a desk. The pace of her immediate computer task quickened as Danny stepped quietly through the doorway. Fingers drummed on keys as fast as five people beating bongo drums. Stopping, her tanned neck craned her tapered nose toward him.

"I-" he squeaked out. Wondering where to start, his

mind searched for a response to her dilating retinas that filled in the light blue in her eyes. A lump in his throat formed. Clearing his throat, he began again. "I'd like to go to South America."

Displaying large white teeth, she pulled large luscious lips back into a smile. Her long fingers drummed on the keyboard as she pulled up new files. "Which part?"

"Bolivia," replied Danny. "By boat?" Wondering how tough the question, he raised his eyebrows questionably.

Her long fingers hesitated. In an encouraging pearly white smile, her bright orange lips nearly touched her diamond studded earlobes. "Cruise," she asked, "for two?"

He shook his head and a sharp pain of remembrance slashed through his forehead. Cutting a defiant grin, he held back the urge to shout at her. To kick her desk! He wanted to tell her the main reason he wanted to travel was to forget the last ten years of his rotten marriage. Especially how his wife had sat around, filling her face. Everything he had tried to get her to move failed. Eventually, he had given her all his money, which he'd inherited and the empire he'd built, just to be left alone. Wanting to wash his hands of it, he wanted to tell the travel agent everything. He decided to bite his tongue. Through clenched teeth, he whispered hoarsely. "I'm alone."

"Looking for a singles' cruise then, huh?" Her teeth sparkled whiter than her glistening white monitor did. "You can meet lots of other singles."

Clamping his teeth tightly together, he puckered his lips and pushed the air out. As though something stank, he crinkled his nose. Then at the top of his exhalation, his mouth unlocked. "No."

She giggled. "I understand."

"Yeah," nodding, he replied, "I just want to get away." Drawing a little breath, he realized how common his problem was. "I plan to work and prospect for diamonds. I want to leave as soon as possible. I'm on a very limited budget. Will it be expensive?"

"Interesting," she replied. "I'll try to find you something cheaper, perhaps a cancellation--" Hesitating, she fiddled around with her computer.

Sweating, Danny nodded. Looking at his arm and leg, he speculated the price. "It's a question of how soon can I leave."

"On an economy cruise," she started, "I can fast track you there by air. Plan B sounds better--."

"No thanks," he interrupted. "I'll stick to my plan." Stifling a laugh, his chest heaved. "There's no two ways about it. Airplanes terrify me. I like to play it safe, keeping closer to the ground. Please, just get me a ticket. The sooner I leave the better."

Two

Black skies screened the midday sun. Wind torrents pushed dark saltwater, creating great crests and peaks. The ocean liner sailed slowly southward through rough Pacific waters. In a split second, a colossal wave knocked the huge white and blue ship sixty-five degrees off course. Standing in his cabin's doorway on the passenger vessel, Danny listened to the captain's update on the vessel's intercom system. Through the noise of whistling winds and of splashing waves, Danny thought that the fellow sounded like everything would be okay.

The captain claimed that everything was all right, and that he expected rough waters. While announcing the new estimated time of arrival to the three hundred sixty three passengers, the soothing voice halted part way into his announcement. A gripping moment of silence followed. A warning bell rang.

"Hurricane bearing this way!" roared the captain. Each word got louder, confirming a cranking up of the amplifier. Speakers crackled in response with distortion. "Turn to emergency channel twelve on your cabin's television set and please remain there until further notice."

Believing other passengers were doing the same, Danny sat quietly in a small cabin glued to the television. Vise-like fingers squeezed the steel bed frame with one hand, while the other gripped the white, emergency suitcase on his lap. With the volume turned up, instructions broadcast abruptly on how to abandon ship. The rocking boat cradled a sensation of terror in his stomach. A full-course vegetarian lunch special sat untouched on a small table beside his bunk. Gulping in fear, his bobbing Adam's apple responded with rancid-tasting gastric acid. Reflecting on his safety, he remembered that there were a lot of lifeboats nearby.

While the calm, young woman on the TV screen explained the contents of the survival suitcases assigned to each cabin, schematics of exiting procedures flashed in and out of the screen like commercials flashing quickly between plays of a Stanley Cup game. Danny knew a pre-recording when he saw one. Feeling certain a cruise line only played them when in imminent danger, he suspected the ship reached the point of no return.

Now he knew why the bargain ticket deal on the Spring Special Cruise was loaded with extras. He'll fly next time, he thought.

Danny placed the suitcase beside him on the bolted-down bed.

With diamond exploration on his mind, he had set out to Bolivia with GPS equipment and detailed South American maps. If stranded at sea, he couldn't afford to leave the two expensive magnetometers behind. If necessary, he'd let the large airtight suitcase float behind his lifeboat. He realized that the two battery-packs and a small solar twelve-volt battery charger, also in the suitcase, would come in handy.

Reaching over, he opened the large case and removed the lab top computer's replaceable electrical adapters. After stuffing the space with some corn on the cob, utensils, and garnishes off the lunch tray, he placed the rest of the food in the emergency kit. Afterwards, he pulled the large case near and became a tube head.

While Station Twelve reported that this specific liner could weather most storms, the captain interrupted and replaced the woman on the screen. Appearing flushed, he breathed fast. "Please stay calm." He swallowed hard. "Yes--" Silence followed and then the television went blank.

Danny leapt to the door to listen to anything on the speakers. While his heart rate broke previous records, his ears opened wide.

Nothing!

Screams of a frightened woman began next door. "Help me! Help me!"

Carrying both cases, Danny charged out of his doorway.

Betrayal In Paradise

Three

"What is it?" demanded Danny as he rushed inside. Stopping dead in his tracks, his eyelids dropped at the sight of the naked lady standing by the bed.

At the alarming sight of a man in her doorway, she turned dumfounded. She felt more frightened now than any other time in her thirty-one years of living, but managed to whimper, "Help me."

Setting down his cases, he glanced around the room.

She tasted the salty teardrops cascading off her round cheeks. Through her cries, she watched him move across her messy room toward a pile of clothing on the bureau. Something deep inside of her wished she could wake up and laugh at this predicament. Something deeper swore that if it were a dream, a younger man would've been the one to rescue her.

The man selected a dress and tossed it to her.

She stared blankly while it fell to the floor.

Growling at her, he pointed at it.

Her brow furrowed while she slipped into the garment. Why should she do what he says? Why would a man and not an employee of the cruise line help a total stranger? Especially when she anticipated that he thought her as useful as a sack of hammers. She hurried, blindly doing as told.

Feeling too obese to be likable, she had booked a

low-priced spring cruise in hopes of meeting someone, of getting drunk, and of having a little fun. She had believed that her one-size-fits-all sundress allowed her to disguise as much fat as possible because it fit tightly. Deep down, she had even debated the thought of actually attending the party. Rather than joining others at the main dining hall, she had revealed her shyness to herself when she ordered lunch in her cabin. After undressing for a shower, the boat had shifted more than before; and in shock, she had failed to put on her dress and instead began screaming. Now, like some room service from above, her knight in shining armor had appeared to her distress. She rushed to hide her nude body.

While waiting, he searched the room. Appearing satisfied with everything, he opened her room's mandatory emergency suitcase. He crammed her uneaten lunch of corncobs, a six pack of bottled water, and a small decorative pumpkin inside it. He handed it to her. Motioning with his hand for her to follow, he picked up his cases and dashed through the door.

Right behind him, she glanced back at her possessions. Although recalling a horrible life, she wanted to live. Be happy anywhere. Even with this stranger. A renewed flood of tears followed, only to be surpassed by the torrents of rain splashing on her blood-drained face, as she exited the room.

~ *~

While hurricane winds violently gusted, the ship's cabins began bobbing below sea level. Peering into the storm, Danny saw a colossal, spinning column of water heading towards them. As water flooded the decks, he forced his cabin door closed. "Get under the bunk!"

Beth clambered under the steel-framed bed and stretched out. As he scaled under and pressed against her, her eyeballs goggled in surprise and her pulse pounded in her throat.

Positioning the mattress between their bodies and the bunk, he pressed his palms against his eyes. "Do this!" he commanded. Even to his own ears, he thought he sounded like a madman. "Never pull them away for any reason. Understand?"

Nodding acknowledgment, she settled in. She probably thought that he stressed overkill because he didn't want her to watch any horrible events unfold. She began shaking even more and sobbed in terror. "For God's sake!" he said. "You're not holding your eyeballs in place! You're keeping your face protected. Just do as you're told!"

Resembling a fishing eagle, the black waterspout fished the luxury liner out of the water and elevated it hundreds of feet above sea level. The ship spun vertically, in a southerly direction for miles, causing intense forces to tear apart anything not bolted down. In this zenith of the hurricane's tearing torrents, a vacuum created a jarring intensity that wrenched limbs and eyeballs from sockets from most passengers.

Rolling back and forth under the bed, Danny could feel his eyeballs stretch from their sockets. Pressing his hands hard against them, he hoped the woman did the same. Offhand, he doubted any lifeboats remained intact. Like a breath of fresh air, he recalled reading about how they built these ocean liners into isolated compartments making them impossible to sink. Yet, as time passed, he wondered if this could be the exception. Every second felt like an hour.

A full hour passed before the ship reached the center of the spinning column of water. When it reached the eye of the column, neither water nor clouds made up the core. A sunny peacefulness diffused the rotating ship.

In the calm, it nose-dived toward the water at speeds of over two hundred miles per hour. Portions of the ship torn off earlier followed. The ocean liner hit the water upside down.

Forces tore the ship, literally in half, lengthwise along the side. The bottom half of the ship mangled into the top half. Lower decks crushed upper passenger compartments. The wreckage lunged a quarter mile below sea level. Then it began boring into water, like a huge, spinning propeller. When pressures sprang open doors, any remaining glass, bubble shaped windows shattered. Salt water filled most of the passenger cabins in moments.

In the instantaneous absence of air, some survivors began to suffocate under water. Allaying in remission, the mangled boat twirled slowly underwater as the hurricane passed quickly overhead.

Abruptly, the wreckage surfaced, but began sinking fast.

Moments before the ship settled into the deep, Danny rolled out of the space under the bunk. Pulling Beth out after him, he pried her rigid hands away from her face before he could get her to move. Except for a distant ringing, everything appeared silent.

For now, he could see. His body moved on its own, as if in some distant world. Beth motioned towards Danny's face and he reached up to touch his nose and mouth. Blood! His ears hurt too.

Beth rubbed her own ears, gulping when she noticed the redness on her palms. Staggering forward, her legs gave out. Refusing to move, she fell back on the bed's steel fame. "It's over," she whispered.

Ignoring her, Danny kept moving. Noticing the ship begin to angle, he remembered thinking about how they built these ships to stay afloat. After what it'd been through, he doubted any ship would stay afloat. He picked up one of the four life jackets from the floor. Like the others, its safety hangers had been broken off when the wall had twisted, and they lay strewn around the room. After releasing the safety clamp still on it, Danny put it on. He opened the door and water gushed in. Quickly gathering his two suitcases, he said quietly, "Get your suitcase and follow me."

With her mouth remaining shut, she sat still. Through clenched teeth, she uttered, "Bastard!"

Giving a low growl, Danny was ready to hit her. He didn't have time for her shit. "If you want to stay here and die, go ahead. I won't stand in your way."

Pouting, she got up. Being thrown around by gravity was probably enough. Was it ever going to end? Before she had time to say a word, she put on one of the other life jackets floating close to her. Clenching the remaining survival suitcase with both hands, she scrambled after him. Speaking more to her own self, than for Danny's benefit, she mumbled softly, "I'm Beth."

She trod heavily, on the deck, behind him. An automated television still explaining emergency procedures filtered through the air of an open cabin door.

"Don't look," warned Danny.

She glanced inside. Seeing the eyeless corpse floating around, Beth's eyes returned to the ocean.

As they sloshed through the water, it was evident that the boat was sinking on a downward slope. When the water reached their waists, they placed the airtight suitcase in front of themselves and threw themselves on those small rafts.

Fleeing away from the shifting, creaking ship, they paddled with their hands and kicked with their feet.

Betrayal In Paradise

Four

Buckling metal screeched, piercing the black, smoke-filled air. In the dark skies, lightening fissured while thunder resounded. Throughout the chaos, Danny heard faint human screams biting at him in all directions. Each shriek cut deep inside him, for he understood the hurt of those facing hopeless odds. Having enough to worry about, he fought the currents created by the sinking twisted metal of the once luxury liner. For now, he fought a battle on two fronts, getting himself out and getting Beth out.

Observing her struggling with her survival kit, he evaluated the probability of her surviving as slim to none. Her chunky physique was dwarf-like in her extra-large life preserver, and he concluded he should've selected it himself. While the straps fastened tight at the base, her plump waist barely contacted the fabric. Resembling a shrunken head on top of a tent with hands sticking out, her small chest and head peeked out of the top half of the jacket. Each time she exhaled a breath, she slipped immodestly out of her safety jacket. If it weren't for the current events, he would have found the sight highly amusing.

She was rapidly losing the strength or balance to stay afloat. Her out-stretched arms grasping at the kit kept her bobbing in the waves sufficiently long enough for Danny to rescue her.

Regularly swimming back to yank the safety device further down her body, Danny wondered if he'd ever make any distance from the pulling currents. In hopes of gaining ground, he adjusted the jacket until her right arm went out the same hole as her head. As each large wave covered her from behind, her suitcase pulled her into a treacherous position. She'd lie prone; with her head submerged, her dress pulled back around her waist. Flabby buttocks and tubby legs stuck out of the back-wall of the swells, kicking out at the air. Danny shook his head. What had he done to deserve this? She was just like his ex wife.

When he swam behind her, he pushed down on her bottom and her legs to allow her to breathe. She appeared to take this pandemonium in stride; so, he never suggested otherwise. When she was calm, he felt calm. When she panicked, he panicked. Although it seemed like forever, he deemed it to be a few hours before they were out of the pull of the currents of the ship, and he believed they had swum over twenty miles. In actuality, they'd traversed less than one hundred and fifty feet from the sinking wreckage.

In the calmer water Beth adapted, treading water on her own. At this time, he knew he'd be able to assist others.

"I remember hearing someone calling for help," he mentioned, steering her in that direction. "It's just a stone's throw away."

They located a young woman bobbing in the waves with eyes removed and hanging out of their sockets. Her face and body looked badly beaten. The empty cavities stared at Danny, as if trying to tell him something. The pit of his stomach turned. "Why are her eyes still hanging?" Danny shouted out to Beth. "If they were torn out by the hurricane, they'd be long gone by now. It must've just happened! It could be a gang of thugs behind it." Now, in no uncertain terms, he knew that he must keep an eye out for that new horrible threat.

"Look at her!" Beth screamed. Turning away, she twisted and flung her heavy suitcase. Her free hand slapped at the water, galvanizing with renewed strength, pulling Danny along behind her.

Knowing Beth would toughen up, remain afloat, and stay nearby; he released his grip on her back, before drawing near the sinking woman. He needed to check for life signs, just to be sure.

Partially out of the water he fished her by her hair. He shuddered when he touched her ice-cold skin. Her joints and muscles were already in a state of rigor. The bruises covering her exposed skin looked like knuckle prints. Believing she had died soon after her screams, he wondered how she lasted as long as she did. Looking for answers, he examined her further.

In a semi-flexed right arm, her white fist gripped a life-jacket lace. Odd that she had the life jacket lacing but no lifejacket. He shivered at the thought of how someone or of how some people had beaten up on her and had blinded her. In over her head, he discerned she fought back by gripping the tie string while her life jacket had been torn away. On the other hand, maybe the hurricane and the currents had been responsible for her doom. With the winds picking up, Danny realized he'd better get a hold of Beth before something worse happened to them.

Sticking it out with her, he kept his eyes peeled for survivors for the remainder of the evening and night. The storm propelled them miles away from the wreckage. They found no one. They didn't talk much, but whenever Beth openly questioned their own chances of being rescued, he growled in reply.

The next morning the sun peeked out, giving Danny a sense of direction. Swimming east to southeast, following the wave action, they searched for land.

Betrayal In Paradise

Five

Wild winds waned. Relentless rains rested. Light peeked through black, splitting clouds. Breaking whitecaps created rainbows in the azure waters. In all this crude beauty, Beth felt so small.

Throughout life, she had shown little ambition to do anything, to get a good job, or to make friends. Thoughts about traveling alone and being of little use to the world seemed to catch up to her here. Echoes of how pointless her pitiful life had been bounced around in her head. Being a survivor contrasted any previous objectives. Now, she labored, feeling good about herself, adrift in high seas. In this extreme struggle, she remained upright while so many others had drowned.

She shuddered in remembrance of the dead woman and it spurred Beth to keep swimming, to keep staying alive. As long as she paced herself, she knew Danny would make her toe the line and keep her on track. The problem was, with her tired muscles hurting and cold, how much longer could she stay awake? The day took on a new light when Danny mentioned he heard something.

They treaded water, pushing their three pieces of floatation luggage, towards a man thrashing his arms high in the air.

Staying mostly hidden behind Danny, she observed the fellow calling them over. Believing the young man to be in his twenties and having all his parts intact, she shifted into the open. Within several feet, she braved a physical assessment. Gasping out loud, Beth noticed the strapping arm and ripping chest muscles breaking through the material of his white, soaked shirt.

"Jeez, am I glad to see you!" exclaimed the fellow. "I'm Shorty." Stomach muscles flexed in his life preserver, which opened when he tilted back. Holding the sides apart with his thumbs, he revealed the lack of lacing. "I thought I was a goner in this."

In the split second after he spoke, Beth gulped and swallowed hard. Her spine tingled and breathing increased. Her heartbeat raced, and mouth spit bile. The tone of his voice seemed distasteful and set her senses on alert. A bad character in a television drama came to mind, but she couldn't remember which one. Would the bad taste in her mouth mean something, she wondered?

Having had her wealth of horror lately, she understood that a lot could happen beyond her senses. Could the nausea be unrelated, she wondered? Forcing mouth corners back, her plump cheeks cloaked her ears giving him an encouraging smile.

"Ya, my wife never made it off the ship." Beady eyes glanced back and forth, between Danny and Beth, before averting to the two suitcases in front of Danny. "During the storm, she set out on her own, screaming about a divorce. Her loss and my gain, I suppose. She was the one with the money."

As Beth's skin crawled, she concluded something about this guy just wasn't right. She wondered if timing of the divorce held water. Maybe he had some wicked kind of defense mechanism and was really traumatized but didn't want to show it. Then again, maybe he was the ass she thought him to be. She glanced at Danny for confirmation.

Danny remained unreadable. Motioning Beth to come closer, he reached for her suitcase. After she released it, he wrestled it to perch on his larger case concealing the geophysical equipment. "Well," he said. "We may as well eat now. After that cold night, we better get something into us."

"You have food?" inquired Shorty.

His eyelids vanished and his eyeballs bore into the suitcases. Beth felt powerless and insignificant. Nodding, she retained Danny's first aid case. In the back of her mind she questioned why Danny packed food in hers, and not his own case; and, if he did, why eat out of hers, only.

After popping the two clasps, he opened it and distributed portions of the corn.

"Not much," commented Shorty. A small whitecap knocked the corncob from his hand. He swam a couple meters to retrieve it, and then swam back. After gobbling it down, he threw the stock away. He stared at the other two flotation cases. "Have the other two more food?"

"Safety supplies in one. Expensive geophysical equipment is in the other." Danny elucidated, "We have to stretch out what little we have."

Nodding acknowledgment, Shorty directed their attention to his right by waving and pointing. "I saw something floating in that direction that could be a raft." He added quickly, "I've been trying to follow it. I couldn't catch it in this jacket though. It's too small and hard to swim in."

"Yeah, you'd likely tire and drown," Danny agreed. "Well, it's up to me then." While positioning the three luggage pieces until Beth controlled them, his bloodshot eyeballs fixed sternly on her. "Just stay here. I'll swim around a bit and look for the raft. Maybe you two could switch lifejackets."

While nodding, she noticed Shorty smiling. Knots turned in her stomach. She hoped Danny would hurry back.

In no time long arm strokes eased Danny out of sight.

Shorty quickly discerned Beth's struggle with her lifejacket. He pointed. "I'll take it off and fix it for you."

"No thank you." Moving away from him, her heart beat faster then a hundred drums at a Pow Wow. "I'll do it myself."

"Come on," he coaxed. "You'll be better off." Shifting close to her, he stretched to seize her.

Goose bumps formed on goose bumps in the chilly water. With a trembling hand, she pushed his arm away. When he continued to advance on her, she splashed salt water in his eyes. She could think of nothing else to do, but it was enough of a distraction for her to move away and slightly distance herself from him. "What do you mean?"

Sounding a celebrating, spine-tingling laugh, Shorty drove the message home. "There's not enough food for all of us!"

"You bastard!" cried Beth. With high hopes of shortening the time in which he could pulverize her, she shoved the baggage as hard as imaginable. As the bags launched one way, she thrashed the water to propel the other way as fast as conceivably possible.

Shorty advanced as quickly as a shark. Powerful fingers clutched her long locks of bleached hair, snatching her close as he wound her hair around his fist.

Pain exploded in her head. Her body twisted for freedom.

He reached out with his other hand and untied her jacket's lacing. She struggled, trying to shove his hand away. After dislodging her life jacket, he nudged her head underwater. Pulling her up, he twisted her face towards his to look her in the eyes. Coldly laughing at her vulnerability, his pupils dilated as if it were Christmas for him. In a bleak tone, he indicated, "Nothing personal."

As he thrust her under the icy water, she felt his other fingers digging in her eye sockets. Images of the eyeless corpse they'd encountered earlier flashed in her mind's eye. Beth knew she had to act!

Lucky for her, size was on her side. Buoyancy had been troublesome before, but now the water offered little resistance. She stretched out and swiftly kicked Shorty, catching him off guard. Folds of her shoulder length hair extricated from his relenting grip.

In intense pain, she retreated.

Cursing loudly, he swung his fist. It connected with a thump, propelling her further away.

With blood streaming out of her nose, the surge of a heavy ocean wave swept her up. Her purplish white palms dug into the water and pushed. After riding in its swell to a safe interval, she called out in Danny's direction. After one loud scream her voice went hoarse. There was nothing but small whitecaps on the black green ocean. While Shorty peeled off his life jacket, his ominous laugh reached her. Shorty was much larger than Danny was. She was in trouble.

Shorty shucked his jacket and put on hers. "Come on," he coaxed, moving toward her. "You'd be better off underwater."

Beth burnt most of her adrenaline dog paddling to a safe distance from him. She peered in the direction that Danny had gone. She had two choices, calling out or saving energy. Perhaps, she second-guessed, Danny already knew. Thinking better of calling attention to Shorty, she waited.

In time he reached the floating gear. While grasping her bag in one hairy hand, his other thrust the other two bags away. Then he tossed the lace-less lifejacket towards the abandoned luggage. In his get-a-way, he kicked up a small froth of bubbles and waves.

With him safely gone, Beth treaded her way to Shorty's lifejacket. Fortunately, when it had collided with the heavier bag the lighter jacket sprang back. Floating in her direction, it had been easy to reach.

She put on the lifejacket and realized that the luggage was getting away. She had better retrieve them in case they needed the supplies later. She doubted that Danny would locate the raft and knew that it wasn't the time to be a shrinking violet.

Funny, despite doubting she'd exist much longer in this mess, she needed to contribute to life in some small way. She felt obligated to tell Danny about Shorty. In order to reach the bags, she knew she had to give her shit.

Flailing arms raced flapping legs, accelerating her forward. Her huge stomach rolled with each fast breath; holding her afloat. She moved like a speeding water beetle skimming across still water creating large ripples. Catching the retreating bags, she hung on to them and called out.

Danny reached her beckoning cries. "You're bleeding. What happened?"

Beth cried as he pinched her nostrils to stem the flow of blood.

"And that's that," soothed Danny. "It'll be okay."

The bloody nose felt better all ready. She quit bawling. The bleeding stopped.

He unlaced his life preserver and handed the lace to her.

She slipped it in hers. "But the food--"

"What do you think?" He smiled at her. "I'm not stupid. He took the case with the littlest amount of food and left the others. Likely, it's the story of his life."

She should have known better. It had seemed so easy for her mind to make up all sorts of scenarios while away from Danny. With this renewed hope, survival seemed realistic. Yes, if for nothing else, to outlive Shorty and what he represented.

Now, even if Shorty stayed, she reasoned to herself, who really needed the scum? Likely the thief would've eaten most of the food. Who knows what would've happened if the criminal had seen all the food? And why had he tried to gouge her eyes out? What goes on in such an evil mind? Would that be the last of the lowlife?

With all that to think about, she knew Shorty paid the penalty for his lack of patience. Tying up the lacing, she adjusted the life jacket so it fit better than the previous one. Holding back tears, she remarked, "I would've changed him jackets if he'd asked."

"He wanted both the food and the jacket," Danny stated. "Which way did he go?"

"He swam with the waves." She replied.

"The same way we're going." Danny nodded. "He has a good head start, and we'll move slower and search for other survivors. Doubtful, we'll meet up with him again." He turned away from her. Wearing the open jacket, he led them in a south-easterly direction. "Once the waters settle I'll open the larger suitcase and use my maps and GPS." He added, "For now, I'll use the sun's position interpreted by my watch as an indicator."

They swam through rough waters, taking lots breaks and stretching the rations. He encouraged her onwards and nodded approvingly at her efforts.

She thought it better than food.

Six

Beth recalled a line from her school days: 'Water, water, everywhere and not a drop to drink.' Craning her open mouth to the side, she tried to catch raindrops but usually ended up with a mouthful of salt water. As well, heavy successive cloudbursts entertaining black clouded skies dampened Beth's sense of direction. She understood up and down but had a bellyful of this identified destination. To her, the raging brine resembled one large rocking chair going nowhere. But in time, even a rocker ceases.

The waters relaxed and the storms abated during the second night. Life took a new direction. At such a time, Danny opened the equipment suitcase.

Selecting the GPS out of his case, he squeezed the start button. The device resembled an average sized calculator, indicating latitude, longitude, and azimuth of the sun and moon. Then he removed a map and some food. After studying it, he placed the diagrammatic representation of their area back and closed the lid. Within a few minutes, the GPS display indicated locating three orbital satellites and a fixed position. He entered a destination. A dot acted as a finger, pointing to a bearing seventy five miles away. Turning the unit off, he laced its string through the life jacket lace holes. Then, they divided the cherished diet, saying as little as possible. Treading water, they floated in the direction indicated by the readout. The waterproof direction finder bobbed alongside the secured life jacket at his chest level. He stayed alongside Beth at a leisurely pace.

Feeling numb, she kicked and paddled in the water as much as possible to keep her circulation going. When she could, she napped during the warmer daylight hours when it seemed safer.

Through the short stints of sleep, she was thankful Danny held his expressionless eyes on her. While he slept, she repaid his kindness by telling him wild lies about her almost being the Queen of England. As long as he grumbled a response or snored, she knew he was alive.

At times she wondered if he comprehended as much as he claimed. When he mentioned relying on the wind and wave direction or the sun's position to relative time, she got confused. The North Star she understood; however, as she searched the dark skies for it, all she saw were stars. It seemed to work just fine for Danny though, as he could easily point at it. Throughout the day she threw all sorts of questions and open concerns about the GPS, trying to remind him he had it, hoping he'd use it more often. He seemed to want to use GPS unit as little as possible, but often reassured her they traversed a straight vector towards Columbia's mainland.

Likely from the salt intake, her back teeth always seemed to be floating. She had to distance herself from Danny to try relieving a non-existent buildup of urine. It occurred to her that the more she deviated away from the course that the more of a chance of attracting a shark. Thinking of sharks kept her shuddering in the seawater. Adding fuel to the fire, her nose failed to heal and bled occasionally sending out her scent.

Plus, making it worse, it was that time of the month. She felt too frightened to mention any of it to Danny. To calm herself down, she thought about the rainy Vancouver coastal days and how she had managed to duck indoors and stay dry. The rainy day thoughts ran wild in her mind, in some sort of looping stress, and she realized she had begun to lose her mind. Superceding the ramblings of her mind, she debated whether sharks smelled or tasted blood. Actual time passed slowly. Minutes seemed like hours. Hours seemed like days. Days seemed like weeks.

The sun peeked over the horizon on the fifth day, radiating friendly rays of hot sunshine. In the blink of an eye, black clouds became white mists before disappearing into a circular, blue hue around the rising sun.

Blinking brutally through the stinging salt water, she gazed at the enjoyable sunrise. It seemed so bright and perfectly warm. In her delusional state, she believed it would immediately set into darkness. When it didn't, she wondered if she was off her rocker. She closed her eyes. Where had she found the strength to come so far? What she had left for tears streamed in this tired state.

The sun appeared to be something bringing a new life, and she wondered what sort of a life. She felt good. It seemed like things were looking up, yet she finally found the strength to end her life in a peaceful way. To hell with it all! It was now or never. She quit kicking and crawled up onto her suitcase, waved goodbye to the world, then slid off. She went straight down, letting go of the suitcase. Looking like death warmed over, she forced a greeting smile. She cared little what happened next.

Something touched the bottom of her bare foot, and her mouth opened in a silent scream below the surface. She clawed at the water, shooting upward. Bobbing out and grappling the top of her suitcase, she scrambled for balance with a renewed hope for living. She fought for a hold, while Danny laughed. Growling at him, her red bulging eyeballs glowered in an insane disbelief. "Danny--"

"That's the fastest I've ever seen you move." A large grin overtook Danny's face.

"Something grabbed my feet." She fought to stay on the floatation case.

"What's that?" Danny's eyebrows quirked and he peered into the water below. "Hey! There's a lot of seaweed and grass floating around here. It means land! This is your lucky day."

No, it wasn't plant life. Plant life didn't move that fast. Beth scanned as much of the area as she could as fast as she could. Soon she saw something in the water. Her body began to shake. She screamed and pointed. Recalling all the bleeding, she wondered if they were always stalking and waiting until the smell induced total madness.

"I see it too!" shouted Danny, "Land!"

"Over there!" she screeched. "Look a bit closer!" Why didn't he understand? She searched for a way to explain, while he talked about land. It would be just her luck to get eaten by a shark after all she'd been through, and now, in sight of land.

Danny peered in the direction of a couple of fins, side by side, advancing quickly on their position. "Now I see!" He shoved her forward. "Head that way. That looks like land. I'll be right behind."

The fins moved behind them.

Positioning himself between her and the fins, Danny followed her closely. When the fins split up, he raised his fist into the air. "Come and get it!"

Doubtful the shark would go away and thinking that Danny was crazier than she was, worked Beth into a fit of frenzy. Quick breaths turned into gasps. Losing her wind, she felt helpless. To relieve any constrictions, quicker than a knife slicing through soft butter at a free food picnic in downtown Vancouver, she peeled the life jacket free. While her small arms tried to keep her body upright, her efforts seemed hopeless. Each time she began to sink, stubby legs managed to kick her pear shape bottom upward.

Swinging at a fin flashing by, Danny bumped into Beth. Wrapping his arms around her backside, he shoved her behind him. "Come and get me!" he cried out. "I've already been to hell!" When the fin came at him he managed to get a hold of something. He hung on for awhile before it slipped away.

Ahead of him, the huge beast advanced on her. "Beth!" he yelled, swimming after her. "Good God!"

Beth wondered if Danny had tried pushing her away to feed her to the sharks. She closed both her mind and her eyes.

The monster bumped her, pushing her back, before pausing.

Cracking her eyelids, Beth peeped at the snout almost touching her face. Blood pounding through veins primed Beth's renewed energy level to explode. Splashing the creature, her arms flailed in the water. Concentrating her movements on the imminent danger, trying to keep upright seemed secondary. Sinking underwater, she swung her fists for protection. When she gasped for air in the water, it felt like sucking in a solid brick wall. A poking sensation rammed into her back.

Surfacing, she glided on the water with one fin in the back of her and another alongside. Puzzled, she doubted she was a feast for their younger ones at home. Trying to recall any instances of this form of feeding happening to anyone, wild animals and pizza delivery came to mind. Experiencing drowning earlier, an easier way to the undiscovered country, to be more painful than everyone claimed. Now, she hoped for a quick death. Unfortunately she'd probably be eaten slowly because of all the fat, and it'd be painful; yet, she took advantage of the air, breathing free and easy. After fifty feet, she started to sink. Going with the flow, the other fin took over and she surfed again. Taking turns, they moved her about a mile before releasing her.

Assuming a ready stance, she braced herself for a fight. In disbelief, her foot touched something solid. Attempting to half swim and half run on the reef, her hands pulled at the water. Suddenly, her feet lost footing. Feeling the reef bar deepen, she recalled the opportunities she could've had to enroll in swimming lessons. She cursed loudly at herself for being lazy. However, with sharks on her tail, she swam as if in the Olympics.

Their long, beak-like snouts paralleled her, making sounds as though trying to speak. At the familiar soothing sounds of dolphins, her tired body relaxed. At the thought of friends, a window of realization opened.

Feeling faint, her head sank in the water until the lack of air jarred her mind. Her fingers clawed at the water until her lungs gulped the surface air. After deep breaths, a horrible taste accumulated in her mouth. She started to vomit. Slime ran out her mouth, sticking to her hair. Her arms moved as pistons, keeping her head higher than her backside. Eventually she reached a reef and waited.

Danny stayed put for a long time. Beth waved her arms, motioning him to get closer. Eventually, he gathered all the cases and her discarded lifejacket and worked his way to her.

She kept shouting, "They are dolphins from the family Delphinidae."

Waving a hand, Danny returned an acknowledgement. It took a long time to get to her position. After looking around, his cracked lips smiled. "We're here," he cried. "We made it!"

With each breath, Beth tasted fresh bouquets of plant life odors. When her eyesight cleared, a half-moon shoreline of a bay appeared in the distance. Each time her feet stepped down and touched the sharp coral reef in those shallows, she cried in joy.

They swam toward shore, when necessary, with the

dolphins swimming circles around them. Beth thought that the dolphins seemed as happy to see them, as she was happy to see land. They must like to meet new friends too.

Betrayal In Paradise

Seven

Things were looking up for Danny. Warm water washed against his cramped legs. Elevating him upright, they performed with a painful, prickling sensation. Sore nostrils sniffed approvingly at the propitious air as exotic breezes permeated his nose, exhibiting wafts of thriving flora with hints of rotting fish. Through a film covering his eyeballs, he saw a blur of piebald earthy greens blending with sandy whites. Dulled by water in his ears, he heard the sharp agitation of birds chirping and the constant chatter of monkeys clamoring. His mind reeled at their dreamlike announcement of his arrival. Touched in the head from lack of sleep, he searched for reassurance that land really existed. He knew it the moment his bare feet touched a soft carpet of sand instead of the sharp corral bottom. Followed closely by Beth, his exhausted body tugged two suitcases onto a sandy shoreline.

Setting the suitcases on the beach, he found some suitable bushes and dashed behind them. Besides screening his actions, the bush's green barrier allowed Beth the privacy she might require. After relieving himself, he knelt down near the puddle. Aching, numb fingers bulldozed sand towards the urine. Having had only short naps since the boat, his vibrating body longed for rest. He could hear Beth's slow deep breaths turn to snores from the other side of the brush.

Before his blistered eyelids closed, the last thing he saw was the sand covering his urine stain.

~ * ~

Hours later, he stopped shivering and woke. Sweating in the heat had kept his clothes wet. Wet fabric clinging to raw skin caused an antagonizing itch. Moving to the brush, he liberated the red nylon jacket and black polo shirt in one jerking movement. After hanging those items on some branches, he realized that the coating covering his eyes had cleared. It took a mere glance to determine a lack of civilization. Although the land went on as far as he could see; yet, he doubted that they were on the mainland. He bolted over to the suitcases.

Removing his maps and GPS, he cross-referenced the positioning system's readings with a large-scale map of the highest quality. He praised himself for acquiring the coastline map as well as many other detailed inland maps in advance. This land set, catching the corner of the map, at which place only water supposedly existed. With the handwriting on the wall, he determined they had a ghost of a chance at being rescued. The sun blazed directly overhead, so he judged it noon. The GPS verified it was 12:15 p.m., May 3, 2000.

They had been floating for almost five full days. Glancing towards Beth, he understood that the resounding snoring and the relentless shivering confirmed her lack of sleep. Thinking about food, his stomach turned. Bushes in the distance would do the trick. His bowels almost let go. Bending forward, he dashed madly until it became a futile effort to reach the thicket. While in full stride, he pulled his pants down. Crouching, he let loose. Five days in the icy water and food shortage had restrained the bowel contents. He glanced over at Beth.

Two round eyes gawked back.

Danny flexed his anus as hard as he could and

dashed for brush cover before defecating again. After scraping clean with a large, dried palm leaf, he buried the evidence and planned to stay out of Beth's sight for ten minutes more. Soon, he heard footsteps moving fast. Knowing she may be having the same problem, he sat down ashamed. After ten minutes, he shook the underbrush and stepped into the clearing.

She had cleaned the area and stepped out of the water, waving to Danny.

After nodding back, he ambled around the immediate area. As far as he could tell, the visible obsidian and lava indicated volcanic actions had built this area. Turning around a large brush, he glanced around. His mouth almost hit the ground at the sight of all the fruits and berries in the area.

After the scarcity of cuisine offered at sea, he fantasized about shopping in a strip mall. Tasting a bit of everything, he became aware of Beth gobbling down raspberries like nobody's business. He felt surprised she got near him so soon. Had so much time passed as he ate, he wondered? Finding a pineapple tree, he settled down in its shade and broke open a fallen pineapple. Wiping sweat from his forehead, he thought about the playful dolphins and wondered how long had they been here. With that thought, he forgot about everything else except munching on the golden, juicy flesh.

Beth ambled over, her feet dragging when she walked.

"You're sluggish as hell. Have a piece of fruit." Danny held out a chunk of the large fruit. He hoped to let her rest a bit before giving her the straight goods about being on an uncharted island.

She readily accepted the fresh pineapple portion. "Let's go find someone. I'd like to go home."

Danny agreed, hoping to get the lay of the land.

Anything sounded better than sitting around. "Feel up to walking around?"

She nodded.

"Please eat first," he said. "I'm going to check my equipment, okay?" As he stood, his tired legs cramped. Kicking the stiffness from them, he hopped toward the suitcases. It was kind of funny, actually. He pulled one side of his cracked lip into a wide grin and directed it at Beth. He warned, "Better keep moving around."

Getting up, she smiled in acknowledgement and turned away from him.

Opening the luggage, he sought out the empty water jugs and GPS unit. He was probably going to be using the solar battery charger lots, so he checked it over and found it intact. Exposed to the sun, the gauge showed a positive charge. In the safety bags, he glanced at the two flashlights and hoped the bulbs would hold up. The rechargeable batteries powered enough voltage to drive the flashlights as well as other equipment for quite some time. After feeding his position into the GPS, he dressed and stashed the suitcases behind some bushes. Placing the two empty water jugs under his left arm, he let the GPS unit dangle off a string around his neck. Exiting the clearing, noted as location 1, he kicked some sand over his earlier droppings.

Following closely, Beth remained silent. She seemed fixed on where she walked and too bashful to glance at his movements. After all, she had only bare feet, he concluded, and must watch where she stepped.

~ * ~

They trekked southward along the white sand, over multicolored rock formations, along the coastline. They crossed marshlands and swamps, indicating land just below sea level, until they scoped a narrow river feeding the ocean. The mouth of the river set at the southern-most tip; so, Danny entered the location in the GPS, editing the point to read southern-most-point. The GPS indicated that reading sat 0.85 kilometers from location 1. They advanced upstream, setting foot into the jungle interior.

"Talk about a variety and a half of colorful vegetation." Attempting to emphasis what he detected, Danny craned his head from side to side in awe. His mouth watered at the kaleidoscopes of juicy, reddish berries blanketed by lush, greenish foliage. Sweet fragrances of berries and fruits complimented the visual splendor of plants, of trees, and of vines. "Some of this stuff isn't indigenous to the region. Seeds were probably brought over from land masses, throughout the centuries, by ocean currents and wind action."

Beth shrugged.

Danny stopped walking as realization struck. "Listen Beth, let's face facts," he said softly. "I should've told you earlier. We landed on an island, far away from anyone. Getting found by a search party is possible but unlikely. On the bright side, we have to be grateful of all the natural food here. The island is a product of volcanic actions. Ironically, my hobby is prospecting volcano vents for diamonds."

Her face paled; her eyes withdrew, but she continued her quick pace behind Danny.

Resting at a small, sandy-bottomed lake, which fed the river, Danny ambled closer and knelt for a closer view. He turned to Beth. "Looks like grayling of sorts." He stood. "I wonder how they got here. Perhaps they were here for a very long time. Perhaps their life originated here, and life still is originating and evolving uninterrupted here."

Beth hunched down. Leaning over, she cupped some water in her hand and lapped it up.

"Perhaps--" he stopped, heeding the far away look in her tear-filled eyes.

Scooping more water, she rinsed her face.

"You hardly scared the fish," Danny observed aloud.

"Why should I?" exclaimed Beth, bluntly. Leaving the bank, she sat down on some course, brown sand while tears slowly made their way down her cheeks.

"It's not that..." Danny hesitated. "It's just that the fish seemed oblivious to movement close to them. Usually, they move quickly away. They must've lived in a world barely threatened by outside influences." Beth didn't seem to appreciate nature the way he did. He changed the subject. "It's time to eat."

"Are you going to scale them?"

"Jeez!" Turning pale, he grew weak. "Let's leave the little fishes alone, okay? I'm a vegetarian."

Her face clamped up, as if downing a pail of sweet and sour sauce followed by pickle juice.

Wandering over to a nearby banana tree, Danny pulled a bunch free and offered some to Beth. She hurried to receive them, appearing to forget everything else. They ate in silence and then set out scouting the land.

They scaled the highest pitch of the only two clear peaks on the island. Danny glanced at Beth. With her mouth agape and dullness in her eyes, Beth acknowledged her isolation in the panorama. Even sighting a few bighorn sheep and white tail deer on the other peak failed to get any response from her. At sunset, they headed backward, to their initial point on the beach. New white clouds seemed to form each time Danny looked up.

While constructing a gigantic bonfire, they stacked huge piles of dried wood for reserves. Beth chose mainly driftwood.

The silence stretched out between them until Danny couldn't take it any more. "Let's leave the driftwood alone next time, huh?"

Beth didn't respond. Instead, she sat by the crackling flames and pulled her knees into her chest. Tightening her lips, she responded with a cold stare into the fire.

He decided to give her the straight dope. "This island is not chartered on my map. Nobody knows about it." Upset at himself for being so blunt, he picked up a fat log and pitched it into the flickering fire.

Sparks shot up into the black sky, only to noisily fizzle out in the damp air.

Beth began to shake. If she started bawling, he knew that she could be real trouble. "Perhaps someone will spot it." He added, encouragingly. "Some big exploration companies use satellite viewing."

Large round brown eyes squinted and full lips puckered, revealing large rounded white teeth. Her cracked voice was barely audible. "Did any others make it? How many others made it?"

"Don't you get it?" Instead of punching something, mainly Beth, he threw another log into the fire. "They are all gone!"

The flames ceased for a few seconds. "Teak wood," he said calmly. Sniffing at the aroma, he put his face into some thick smoke. With it stinging his eyes, he remembered the awful screams. Could he have done more? When the wood caught and flared, he spoke softly. "That should burn a long time."

"Could you've saved more of them if not for me?" Beth asked quietly. Closing in to the warmth of the fire, she placed her shaking palms low to face the fire. Even with the warm breeze off the ocean, she shifted near the fire as if winter winds wailed.

His stomach turned as he swallowed some smoke. He glanced over to the ocean, wanting to close his eyes and cry. "Lots of lives were wasted. We tried to save more. Were some your friends?"

"No." Beth shivered. "I came alone." After a few moments, she added, "More company now would be nice."

"Hundreds more could fit comfortably on the island." His heart raced at the thought of being stranded with a few hundred women, serving his whims. Glancing at Beth, he changed his mind. He found it hard to fathom one Beth, let alone hundreds. Averting his gaze back to the fire, he added, "We could use some shipbuilders and winemakers."

"I'd rather be in a dugout canoe with you, knowing where I'm going," commented Beth, "than drunk on a ship with shipbuilders and winemakers, not knowing where I'm going."

"Thank you." It was nice to hear stuff like that. No one had ever really depended on him before. However, he had enough small talk and got up to saunter over to a suitcase. He pulled out a spare, clear plastic jogging suit jacket, which he kept with his equipment for extremely cold days. "Try this." He handed it to her. "It's pretty thin. I would have given it to you earlier, but it may have made staying afloat more difficult."

Nodding graciously, she accepted the XXL suit and slid into the pants as if tailor-made. "Thank you Danny."

"Some small plastic tarps I use for covering some of my equipment are here too." He reached into the cases. "I'll keep one to sit on while I keep the fire going, and you can use the others to cover the ground. Even beside the fire, you'll have to think warm to stay warm. Tomorrow we'll make a couple of beds, huh?" The alternative thought of having to hug her all night, to keep her warm, sent a chill through him. Picking another log, he threw it into the blaze.

She fell asleep instantly and snored loudly.

Shivering from fatigue, he felt too tired to sleep. After throwing some large logs in the fire, he pulled his arms to his chest and tried to understand the fickle finger of fate. It escaped Danny how Beth entered the big picture. Losing his train of thought, pebbles seemed to scrape the insides of his raw eyelids as they closed. Soon, he fell asleep sitting up and hunched over against a rock.

~ * ~

The following day, Danny's fingers probed into the ice cold water streaming out of the ground on the other immense peak. His free hand pointed down the hill. "Three artisan wells feed that small lake out of this mountain." Gesturing his finger to the small river, he added, "Must be others right under the lake and around it to make as much water as that river displaces. The water seems to pulsate." He shrugged. "It's likely caused by wave action pushing against the island. Because of all the volcanic action, the vent is stable, but the sand built up around it moves and acts like a pump. With the sand filtering the water, and has been for a long time, we'll have plenty fresh water."

Cupping some water, she lapped at it. The noise stirred something behind her. A curious brown rabbit hopped closer.

"Wild rabbits usually fear humans." He recalled seeing lot of tracks. "Most of them swam over here and bred," he surmised. "Perhaps others swam off ships sunk by pirates."

Beth nodded. "Perhaps they were sunk by storms." Her bloodshot eyes searched the area. "Are you going to hunt?"

"I'm a strict vegetarian." Thinking that perhaps she planned to hunt on her own, he glared at her and frowned with his wrinkled brow.

"Vegetables are okay by me too, I guess."

He pointed west. "Feel up to it?"

Beth nodded. Her face was sullen and he though she might cry. Deciding to remain quiet about the wildlife, he chose to walk along the sandy shoreline.

She followed slowly behind.

After hitting the island's western point, Danny

pressed the GPS coordinates in.

Drawing large breaths, Beth shrugged her sweating shoulders. Glancing about, she wiped moisture off her face and sat on a log.

Seeing how worn out she looked, Danny turned away and inhaled a long breath. Jeez, the ocean air tasted great and the inland scenery was breathtaking. A lot of thick bush blocked lower countryside and looked like tough sledding. Making up most of the island, the two mounds appeared worth investigating. They reminded him of something. Rather of something someone lacked. He glanced at his companion. "Do you feel like scouting or making camp?"

"I'm tired." She added, "I think we're here for awhile."

They headed back to set up a camp.

~ * ~

The sun crept to the ocean's horizon, slowly casting ray after ray of light. It wasn't long before the day woke Danny.

After throwing in logs throughout the night, he huddled near the smoldering fire with drawn up knees. Tired eyelids open, and he glanced over at Beth, several feet away, to check out her state. Each time she shivered, he had thrown another log on the fire. Now, snoring selflessly, everything seemed all right.

A hump beside Beth moved slightly.

Danny's heart sped up, and he shook the sleep off his body. "Beth, stay still," he whispered, hoping to wake her gently. "Beth, wake up. It's important."

The loud snoring stopped, but her lids remained shut.

"Looks like some giant spider beside you."

Two reddish eyeballs goggled upwards.

"Take a second to wake up, then jump to your left

and roll."

Beth attempted to leap to her left but could only twist away.

The creature turned and leaped. He stopped after two leaps and croaked.

"Ouch," cried Beth, and her hand went to her jaw.

"Only a giant toad," said Danny with a laugh. He knew that Beth had bitten her tongue, stopping any screaming. "You're a lucky woman. He probably sat there most of the night and ate any bugs heading towards you."

"That was big of him."

"Your snoring must've out croaked him." Danny attempted a sincere tone. "The heat and light off the fire must've attracted him too."

Moving away gingerly, she glanced around the area where the frog had sat.

Leaping up, Danny laughed as he landed on all fours. Hopping towards some bushes, he said, "Well, we may as well make a hut."

"Ha! Ha! Funny!" She sneered, "Wait till it happens to you." Getting to her feet, she watched the toad leap behind some thick underbrush of climbing wild pea shrubbery. A sigh left her lips and her shoulders dropped. After shaking and stretching her fingers, she bent over her suitcase. Fumbling around, she pulled out the slim remains of a corncob.

"Better save and plant what's left," he stated flatly. "Some of it may still seed." Disappearing behind the bushes, Danny reflected that they could be there for a while. "Beth, give me a hand cutting branches and leaves for a hut."

After placing the corn back in the case, she headed towards Danny.

"Beth, we have to talk." Pulling on some palm leaves of a short palm tree, he nodded when she pulled on one on the other side. "I don't know how to tell you this."

Trying to choose his words, he worked slowly on the branch. He looked down towards his feet. "We're going to be here for awhile. I like it here but you don't. I'm wondering what to do with you.

"What do you mean?" Tears formed in her eyes, and she began to shake. "Where am I supposed to go?"

"I don't know." Shaking his head, he kept his eyes fixed on his bare feet. "The way you complain sometimes. Even when you keep quiet, I can see it in you. You make me feel like my life is over."

"I can't help it," she sobbed. "We may never get rescued."

"You're complaining again. I just left behind someone like you. I couldn't stand her."

"Who was she?'

"I'd rather not think about her." He shuffled his feet. "She was just someone who turned out to be too much upkeep. Everything was about her. I could win a million dollars and she'd find something to complain about. I don't know if I could run around, trying to make you happy someplace you're not."

You're happy here."

"I'm alive." He looked out over the ocean. "This place is paradise to me. I don't want anyone to ruin it."

"How can I change?"

He looked at her. "You can work and pretend to be happy. Your life is more important than my prospecting for diamonds."

"Do you mean it?" She leaned closer.

"Well," he hesitated and put his hands behind his back. "Yes, of course."

"I'll pull up my socks," she said. "Just let me try to pull my own weight. Help me build my own cabin. I won't bother you."

"Really," he said. "You'd be okay with that?"

"Yes," she replied. Her trembling stopped. "Answer me one thing."

"Okay."

"Were your fingers crossed when you had your hands behind your back?"

After a slow, short laugh, he looked at her and smiled. "Yes. But I did it in case you started crying and complaining too much. I had to try to make you laugh."

"You're too nice," Shaking her head, she smiled. "I meant what I said."

"Good," he said, "We'll make a hut. It wouldn't be the first time, but if I leave, no hard feelings, huh?"

"Maybe someday you'll tell me the whole story," she said. "But if you leave, I'll understand. You wouldn't be the first I chased away."

While searching for dried bamboo, trees, and vines, Danny called her over again. "I decided to make camp at the shoreline to search for others and for ships. We stayed here already and could always carry fresh water. What do you think?"

"I think it's a good idea," she said. "While you're out prospecting, I can gather a lot of food."

The camping ground shaped up fast. By noon, they completed the lean-to and the framework to expand it into a large room. After filling water jugs and gathering wild fruits, they set about building a signal fire. The extra work of finding dead woods rather than using driftwood took extra time. He saw she seemed docile to it.

Afterward, they traversed along the shore to the eastern point. Along the way, they stacked woodpiles to create a chance for rescue. If necessary, they planned to light the whole works at once.

"At its widest point," mentioned Danny. "The land is two thousand nine hundred fifty three meters east to west."

When they retired for the day, both fell instantly asleep. When they awoke, the toad sat beside her. Between her fits of giggling, she said, "Thank you it for your protection, Mr. Frog.

~ * ~

The following day, while trekking along the northwestern shoreline, Danny pointed to mounds, side by side, of approximately the same dimensions. "Some sort of tombs?" he thought out loud. "Man made or alien. Maybe even from some Inca ruler."

"Inca, you're kidding?"

"They were the civilized rich of three hundred fifty years ago or so."

"Civilized?"

"They ruled by making everyone work."

"Rich, you said?"

"Could be buried treasure," mentioned Danny.

"Is that what civilized people did?"

"They took the money with them."

"Are you going to dig it up?"

"It belongs to historians," he commented. "Let them dig it up. On second thought, I'd rather if no one touched it."

"What makes you think it's anything."

"That would explain all those animal tracks." As well, he recalled some of the strange monkey sounds he'd heard since he had stepped foot on the island. He elaborated, "Respected ruling classes may've brought part of their stocks here. We'll never know what we run into. On one of the peaks, I saw some bighorn sheep and white tail deer. Those are from North America. I'm uncertain what South American animals look like. For all I know, some species we could find may've had been on the verge of extinction or rare. Perhaps this was a way to pay nature for what they took. By letting the animals multiply assured the travelers food during their next visits."

"Lots of animal tracks," agreed Beth.

"Lots of lush vegetation," added Danny. "Almost as thought there were gardeners here."

At the far corner of the island, they lit a signal fire using mainly green logs. After it was smoking well enough, they left. On the way back Beth told him how much she missed her house in Vancouver.

Remaining indifferent, he cared little about Vancouver and said nothing. For now, his mind focused on the type of rocks lying around. Glassy, greenish kimberlite, the diamond host volcanic rock, glittered everywhere. The glistening sand seemed peppered with diamonds.

At camp that night, he lay with his head against a log, looking at the stars, happy with his find. Glancing at Beth, he hoped that she would come to grips with living on a deserted island.

She sobbed herself to sleep.

Eight

Beth's heart beat as rapid as pounding drums in a heavy metal band every time Danny came near. Temporarily filling her lonely void, she even liked his grubby smell. After all, men wearing some sort of after-shave cologne dropped her like a hot potato even before the date. With her it had been leave-em, rather than love-em and leave-em. If she could've learnt to like herself, maybe others would've had liked her. In response to their unflattering remarks, she had pitied them and had thought herself to be more genuine than them. For her, things began looking up when thoughts of her life in Vancouver seemed distant and not missed.

Without question, she knew Danny loved it here. She hoped he had an inkling of how much she liked him. Maybe, in time, she'd grow on him. She expected to be stranded for at least a month. Who knows, she fantasized, after thirty days, she might have to beat him off with a stick. Having heard stories about male testosterone, she had moaned at each new version of the thought.

While helping out, she noticed his muscles strain. When he maneuvered a large log to stack for the fire pit, she sneaked a peak at him and found their eyes meeting. Blushing, she turned away quickly. He looked nice and nothing special, she thought, but he was the most handsome man on the island. Doing a large chore, she worked her way really close to him. While reflecting on how good her day was going, she stared inadvertently toward his crotch area lost in thought.

"You could go pick berries if you're tired here." With his face twisted as though he would throw up, he looked as though he wanted to beat *her* off with a stick.

Caught, she lost her tongue. As quickly as she could, she averted her stare in the direction of some thicket. *Yes, thank you for saving my life*, Beth wanted to shout. *You are a wonderful man!* She got up, heading towards some raspberry bushes.

"Hey Beth," he called after her. "You can use the plastic covering the magnetometer to carry the berries. Just shut the case afterwards. I'm going to be busy building a boat."

After backtracking to his equipment case, she pulled some plastic out of it. Wondering if he checked out her behind, she wiggled back to the berry bushes. She glanced towards Danny.

Moving some logs about, Danny remained focused on the task at hand.

Having a man so close, but not noticing her as a woman, she pretended that her walking was eye candy to him. Heading to some nearby bushes, she swayed her hips from side to side. Even if it was wishful thinking, she liked to believe that she covered more distance walking that way. After spreading the plastic flat on the sandy ground, she began collecting berries.

She was horrified at the thought of riding on another boat; yet, she felt satisfied in having one nearby. Envisioning herself kneeling comfortably on a dugout canoe with a sail and pontoon for balance while Danny paddled, she could almost taste the salty splash from the ocean against her lips. His knowledge and his equipment made her believe he was her best bet of getting back safely.

After spending half the day dragging logs of various

shapes, sizes, and states, he sat in the shade and stared out over the light blue ocean water toward the dolphins jumping over each other.

Trying to get him to talk and to mind her, she tried a new approach. She complained loudly, "My hands are tired."

Averting his gaze to some trees inland, he inhaled deeply. Turning back to the ocean, he released the whistling air though puckered lips. As her heart raced at the thought of isolating him further, she chattered on. "My knees hurt more."

Gazing at the ocean, he remained silent.

Biting down hard to silence herself, she grimaced. Reaching for her mouth, she stood up and bent over. Through clenched lips she murmured, "Now I've bit my tongue."

Getting up, his eyes remained locked on the ocean.

She started closer. "It's not that bad."

He ignored her and ran towards the ocean.

Following closely, she reiterated, "Really, it's not so bad."

She shook her head in disbelief at being so casually dismissed. After hitting the surf, Danny dove in and swam into the surf.

A lump formed in her throat but she'd be damned if she'd call out. Tears swelled in her eyes as he swam further and further out to sea.

She stood on tiptoes. There was something else in the water. Now, the cat was out of the bag. Rather than sit here listening to her, he'd rather play with the dolphins. She shook her head. One minute he was all work, and the next minute he's out swimming.

Danny reached shore. The object followed closely.

"Oh!" she gasped. Blood rushed through her veins so fast, she felt like she would burst. Panic set in. She bit down hard to prevent herself from screaming. Beating a hasty retreat, she searched for something to hide behind.

"Boy," Shorty gasped as he pulled himself onto the sandy beach. "Did you see the size of those fucking sharks?" He lugged Beth's initial survival pack until dropping it on the sand just past the ridge made by the waves. "I seen your smoke since yesterday, otherwise I would've been lost at sea."

Unmoving, Danny remained silent as he followed the burlier man onto the beach.

Forcefully scuffing her foot in the sand, Beth stubbed her bare toe against a log. Wincing, she glared at Shorty through an opening in the thick underbrush.

"You can only guess how nice a bed in a good hotel will feel." Shorty sat down on the beach.

"This island is deserted except for us," explained Danny. "We're off the ship too." He nodded towards Beth.

Skipping a heart beat, her teeth clamped tightly as if trying to send a telepathic message for Danny to shut his mouth. What the hell was he doing, she wondered? Her heart drummed a mixture of high-intensity acid rock music, and of high-volume, adrenaline filled blood into her exploding head. Rolling further back, she ducked out of sight

With their eyes, both Shorty and Danny searched the area.

The shivering woman cowered behind some greenery, listening as best as she could. Even through squeezed tight eyelids, she could still visualize Shorty standing a good six inches taller than Danny.

"People have been known to do horrible things in desperate situations." Danny said explicitly, as though crudely trying to drive home both a point and an answer. "I'm sure you didn't plan to hurt her."

With a stunned far away look, in his darkish black-brown eyes, he peered calmly at Danny. "You're the ones in the water."

Nodding, Danny turned in Beth's direction.

"I was scared." Shorty explained. "I guess I panicked." With his head drooping dejectedly toward the ground, he held up his right hand as though giving an oath. "I couldn't help it."

Beth gritted her teeth. After that last meeting, Danny should toss him right back into the ocean. Tears welled up in her eyes at the memory of almost drowning.

"I'm tired," said Shorty. He strolled over to a shady area, dropped down, and began snoring.

Danny went back to work sorting out various logs for his raft.

She took short quick breaths. Getting her head together, she took a deep breath, swallowed hard and joined Danny. Even while Shorty slept, she was still afraid. Time passed slowly, driving her to pace back and forth instead of to work. Glancing sideways at Shorty, she realized how exhausted he looked and giggled loudly. It was the first time she'd giggled so uncontrollably on the island, and somehow it sounded out of place. Soon, Danny joined in, and they began to belly laugh.

After releasing obvious pent-up emotions, they went back to work while Shorty slept.

Nine

While Shorty snored up a storm, Beth and Danny set about with their chores. "I think we're safe." Danny said. "Even so, keep your distance while we check out his movements." When Shorty woke and ran out back towards some bushes, Danny added, "Not those movements." Without answering, Beth split in the opposite direction.

Strutting towards Danny, Shorty returned. "Run across signs of anyone?"

"No. No one," replied Danny. "This isn't even on the map. We're one hundred and eighty seven miles away from Columbia's mainland."

Shorty sat down on some sand near some shade. "You know quite a bit?"

"Yeah, I got a GPS and some maps."

He pointed at some logs.

"Building a boat," explained Danny. "We could sure use the help."

"I'm afraid I won't be much help," commented Shorty. He lay back on the sand. "Too tired and cramps coming on. Could you fetch me some water and some food?"

After nodding understandably, he brought him some water but stopped short of food. His arm arced in a one hundred eighty degree angle as he pointed inland. "Walking will prevent cramps. When you're ready to get up, the mall is that way."

Danny sat down. "Listen Shorty," he said politely. "The woman is scared of you. After your stunt in the water, she has good reason to be, and it's going to take some time to earn her trust. And I've been thinking. If you saw the smoke, then someone else could have too; so, there could be more people out there. I'd like to keep the fires burning steadily. You could keep the one on the eastern tip burning. I'll check on you and make sure you're all right. Yes, I'm sure after awhile, Beth will get used to you and see that you mean her no harm." Danny raised an eyebrow as if to say, I'll be watching to make sure you don't.

"I won't be moving right away."

"Sure, rest for now." Danny returned to his boat and signal fire.

Just as soon as Shorty fell asleep, Beth came out of hiding and helped Danny with the boat.

Danny rolled his eyes. "Poor Shorty is too tired to work at saving his own life." Danny stopped and looked at her. "At nights, we'll have to help him to attend the east fire. He's rotten to the core. We can't trust him to keep at it through the night."

"We'll have to try to catch up on our sleep in daylight. At least a fire will smoke a long time."

"Of course," agreed Danny, resuming work. "It's up to us. We have to try to save others. If he saw the smoke, others may see it as well."

~ * ~

After a couple of hours, Shorty awoke and with personal needs to attend, he headed into the thicker brush. Beth went in the opposite direction and waited by a brush line. The moment Shorty came into view, she hid behind some raspberry bushes. Scared shitless, she could feel each beat of her heart. Picking berries, she kept an eye out for Shorty.

He seemed to be feeling better, because he worked on the boat with Danny.

It didn't take very long for Beth to determine that she

had picked enough berries to hold a Ukrainian wedding. She moved to a small clearing and knelt onto the soil. Carefully, she poked a finger into the soil every few inches, creating small holes and planted the corn kernels. With a small hollowed out coconut, she carried fresh water to the newly planted seeds and watered them liberally. Berries were yummy, but she didn't want to live off of them forever.

With that task completed, she decided to find some logs suitable for the boat construction. She pulled at a large dried, dead log partly immersed in some sand. The log freed easily. Enjoying her small victory, she dusted the log off. Then, she remembered Shorty and glanced around. Beginning to shake, she got the jitters. Her top teeth ground against her lower set. Squeezing her eyelids shut, she shut out the panic attack. Glassy eyes stared into blackness and all she could only think about fleeing. With legs racing her mind to shut Shorty out, she ran farther into the island and hid.

With her chest heaving and her heart racing, Beth wondered when she'd have to talk to Shorty. Something physical to do might clear her head; so, she continued her chore, searching for other dried logs. Finding one, she bent over to snap some branches off, but as a shadow moved nearby, her heart almost stopped. She turned around.

"It took me long enough to find you," Shorty said with a cocky smile.

A lump in her throat prevented her from screaming. Instead, neck muscles managed to nod her head. Shrugging shoulders followed. A bad taste in her mouth tightened her lips. Glowering eyes pierced the towering man, seeking signs of sudden movements.

"I just wanted to apologize," he said softly. "I must've been off my rocker when I scared you in the water."

An apology was not what she expected. Beth began to cry.

"I--" Stopping, he looked towards the ocean, where Danny had stopped what he was doing and was now taking large strides in their direction.

"I hope you understand." Shorty's face reddened. Saying nothing more, he stomped towards some nearby logs.

Giving him a glare, Danny passed by closely and stood about five feet away. He glanced back and forth between Beth and Shorty. "Beth," Danny asked, "Is everything okay?"

In a tizzy of breathing hard and of muttering curses, Shorty began tossing the logs about.

"It's all right," she said. "He tried to say he's sorry." She was still scared stiff but she noticed Shorty barely paid attention to their conversation. Instead, he headed back to the boat.

"I'll tell him to keep his distance."

Beth nodded, thankfully. Turning away from Danny, she continued working on the log.

Danny closed the distance between him and Shorty. He rubbed his lower lip thoughtfully. "Listen up," he started. "Beth is really frightened. She wants you to stay away from her. I think you should too. The lean-to on the ocean is all yours." He escorted Shorty back to the raft.

In the evening, Shorty set out for his hut without saying good-bye, a fact not lost on Beth. Still, she wasn't certain that he'd really left so she was nervous about showing Danny where she stacked the logs. They decided to move them another day and sat down in front of the signal fire to talk.

Darkness began blacking out the partly cloudy sky. You never really noticed that one thing in the city. You usually saw a gradual change from light to dark but here there really wasn't much middle ground. Light one minute, glorious sunset the next and then pitch black.

Danny tossed a small branch into the crackling flames.

Sparks shot straight up. The weak breeze lacked the strength to blow them sideways. Both Beth and Danny watched the sparks linger.

"I hope he'll stay away from you now

"Yes, I hope so too." Turning, she peeped over her shoulder into the creeping night. She wondered if she'd get any sleep with him out there.

"You aren't missing anything by not working close to him," claimed Danny. "He's got some sort of rash off the water, making it painful to wash or wipe. He sure smells awful."

Averting her glance downward towards the sand in front of the fire, she cupped her palm over her mouth and giggled.

They chatted late into the night and took turns sleeping.

In the morning, Beth kept to herself except for a small deer that kept her distance until well into the afternoon. When Beth offered her some picked berries, the young animal had stayed away. It had taken hours of Beth's coaxing before she came within a few feet. It was relaxing to know she gained the trust of a wild animal. Besides, Beth was happy to have likable company for most of the day. When the fawn finally drifted away, Beth realized the time and headed back to camp.

Ten

In the evening, Beth appeared by the perimeter where Danny and Shorty labored at constructing the raft. She stood and watched. Danny waved to her.

The movement startled Shorty, who turned toward Beth. At the sight of her, he dropped the log he was dragging, gave it a kick and walked in the direction of his own camp.

"At least he knows enough to stay away from you," said Danny.

"Thank goodness for that."

"He still pretty weak because of the lack of food while in the water. If we're to take advantage of that, we'll have to move fast. If we wait, it could be curtains for us."

"We're living on the edge. What can we do?"

"I don't have a clue."

"We could ask him."

"What? Shorty, please don't go away mad; just go away."

"Without question, we're in over our heads."

Before hitting the hay, Beth and Danny peeled bamboo to make rope to lash the logs together.

The large toad aroused them in the morning with its annoying, constant croaking. Danny's hair stood on end. Something was wrong. "Let's move the stacks of logs you found the other day before Shorty shows up."

"Right on," she said. "I'd rather not have to walk around with him and point out all the dried logs I found and cleaned. Plus, I want to be of some help."

"Will it help put you at ease?"

"I'm so scared." She set out to work. "Anything will help."

On the way, she turned to Danny. "Yesterday, I made friends with a baby deer."

"Wow! Did you get close to her?"

"She ate right out of my hands."

"You sure have a way with the wildlife here. First the toad huddled up to you and now the fawn."

"You forgot the dolphins," she beamed.

"That's right." Danny added, "Animals see inside and look at the inner beauty."

Suddenly, she quit smiling. "Not like people."

Forcing a smile, he knew she was right. It hit home, making him upset with himself for being one of those people.

On their last load, they were on their way back to camp when Danny stopped unexpectedly. He turned in confusion to his companion. "Do you smell that? And why is it so quiet? Even the birds aren't chirping."

"What's happening?" asked Beth. She towed a couple of bamboo logs with a long vine.

"I noticed something earlier." Stopping, she sniffed at the air. "Oh my gosh! Is that meat cooking? He wouldn't!" Dropping her cargo she ran toward the scent.

Releasing his own burden of logs, Danny took off after her. For someone scared to death of Shorty, that woman sure could move in his direction.

Bursting through bamboo, Beth led the way into Shorty's base-camp. Charging into its clearing, she paused midway through her stride and turned. "Oh no!"

In front of her hung a small deer hide.

Beth paled but proceeded ahead. Her hand went to her gasping mouth. She stumbled backward, toward the brush.

On her tail, Danny spotted the small head and tiny hooves a few feet in front of Beth. Flies picked at the blood drops and scattered entrails.

So intent on his work, Shorty failed to realize he had company. He continued cleaving the rest of the meat from the carcass in front of the large signal fire. The bloodied black slab of biotite sliced into the small hindquarter, like a fireman's axe, splattering red juices everywhere. Meat sizzled and popped on a green branch stretched over the crackling flames.

The fumes turned Danny's stomach. He didn't think there was another smell in the world that was worse than roasting flesh, except for maybe Shorty. He stunk badly too. Beth took off, screaming over her shoulder. He expected her to head back to the raft.

Shorty stopped the butchering and looked up. He waved a greeting and indicated his kill. Lifting "Look what I scored," he bragged. "It came right up to me."

Beth reappeared right behind Danny. Standing behind him as though he was her shield, she berated Shorty. "You killed that baby deer. You asshole creep! You are a bastard!"

While she expressed other obscenities vehemently, Danny remained between them and stretched both his hands out to his sides as if to contain and limit her movements. Off to a bad start, he stared at the figure towering in front of him. If Shorty wished to do them in, Danny knew that he lacked the strength to prevent Shorty from doing so. Regardless, he held his ground as Beth continued to expand her thoughts.

Making her point, she waved her straining fists into the air then raised her middle finger before retreating into the bush.

Shorty tightened his lips and glared in Beth's direction. "What's with her?"

"Disappointed, I guess," stated Danny, shrugging and lifting his palms to his sides.

"Typical woman," grunted Shorty. "Can't stomach the kill, but usually is the first at the dinner table." He shrugged his shoulders and turned towards the fire. "Want some?"

"No thanks."

"Why? It's tasty."

"I'm a vegetarian. It must be what got her going," explained Danny. "To top it off, it sounded like she tamed and befriended the fawn you killed." Keeping his eyes trained on Shorty, he searched for some sort of sign.

Clenching and unclenching his free hand, Shorty spoke volumes.

Shorty was already pushing it to the limit. This time was as good as any to finish the discussion they'd started earlier. "She's scared to death of you and wants you gone."

"Sure," he nodded. "I understand. I don't want to be stuck here any longer than I have to." Staring straight at Danny, his large, hairy hand squeezed the large slab of biotite until his knuckles turned white.

"You'll leave soon." Danny knew that Shorty needed him to get off the island. "With the GPS and maps you could make it by yourself," assured Danny. "I'll show you how in the morning. Today, you cook the meat and gather up the rest of the animal and the rest of your belongings. Get everything prepared to move away from here. I'll complete the boat during that time. Once you reach land, you can send someone for us, okay?"

"Fine with me!" Shorty stabbed at the meat in a blinding fury.

Without batting an eye, Danny left the site. He had acted hard as nails, and his cooler head had prevailed.

~*~

With Beth hidden on the north side of the island, Danny furnished Shorty with last minute instructions on the south-eastern side.

"But I'll get lost," complained Shorty. "You should come with me. She could wait here till you send someone back."

"You have the GPS and map." Danny said, "The weather looks fine. You should double-check the vine bonds tying the logs together. Keep to your bearing as much as possible. Try to use the GPS as little as possible to save the batteries. If you get tired, the small bed should keep you dry. Just throw the waterlogged log off as an anchor. The vine should hold in smooth water. You got half of the water jugs, all of the meat, and lots of vegetables."

"You think I should take the whole deer?"

"Well it seems that would really calm down Beth."

"Can't you simply burn the extra?"

"She feels that the death of the deer would be on her shoulders."

"Ha!" Shorty shook his head in disgust. "What the hell!"

"I wrapped the head, skin, and bones in some air-tight plastic separate from the stuff you roasted all day yesterday." Speaking rapidly, he hoped to downplay the situation and keep the upset muscle-bound giant in check. He had a feeling that plastic would come in handy, but to make Beth feel better, he decided to give it up.

To tell the truth, Danny wasn't happy to rid the island of the small dead deer for other reasons. With only a few of them around, he wondered if a balance between animals and predator might exist that he had yet to understand. With a gap in the food chain, humans might be next on the menu. At any rate, he wanted Shorty to leave so bad he could taste it.

"It's not a big deal." he continued. "Just dump it somewhere in the ocean. Seeing how the bag is air tight, it won't attract the attention of any sharks."

"Maybe I won't even throw it off," said Shorty, sarcastically. "I'll keep it as a trophy."

Unmoved by the smart-ass, Danny waved his hand in the air as if to say so long.

"Are you sure you won't come?" Shorty's voice turned sincere. "Two paddles are better than one. We could send someone back for her."

"I have to stay."

"Fine," Shorty huffed. "Who needs you?" After getting up on the raft, he pushed off shore with his long pole. In deeper water, his large, split-in-half, bamboo paddle swooshed in the water and advanced the craft in a successful forward motion.

Danny stood on shore, sweating bullets until Shorty disappeared over the horizon, and doubted he would return with help. The last thing he'd want to deal with would be Beth testifying in a courtroom about how he had taken her life jacket and her food supply. If anything, he'd more likely come back with a rifle.

Regardless, Danny admired him for having the guts to set out alone. Feeling sure Shorty left them for good, Danny focused on making some sort of a life here. A good hour later, he set out to find Beth.

Eleven

Beth tossed all the traces of bloodstains and flesh into the signal fire. "Vegetarian, you bet," she joked. "Where do I sign up?"

"You can sign here." Danny grinned. "I'll certainly be happy." He threw some green elephant grass on the flames to smudge the fire. "That bully was not all there. Someone had to take him down a peg."

"Sure nice to see him gone."

"He should've had the Happy Jack pirate flag flying on his little ship."

Beth laughed and stepped back a couple of steps as a coughing fit overtook her. Smoke spewed out of the fire pit, stinging her nose. "Do you think he'll make it?"

"Sure, but I wouldn't get my hopes up of him sending help."

"No?" she asked. Her face fell. "You don't think so?" She crossed her eyes and blew out a breath, making her lips vibrate.

Danny's belly rumbled. "Yeah, he'll send the cops."

"I'd put my money on the Calvary!"

"Mine would be on a hit man."

Her expression stilled and grew serious. "Let's hope not."

"Yeah," agreed Danny. "But, I think that he'd have enough of sea travel. Even if he remains quiet, they'll figure out that he had to come from somewhere close. Someone will come once they estimate the position that the ship possibly went down. Right now, they're calculating distance versus time."

"So the more days that pass, the wider they'll make the search."

"Bang on!" Leaning away from the smoke, he bent over and picked up a long stick. Holding the butt of it, he stirred the grass to cover some flames before continuing. "But we're quite a distance away from the shipping lanes. With Shorty, the real question is whether or not he'll admit to being on the boat."

She nodded. "More than likely he would seek some sort of compensation from the tourist agency. They could track his movements." Her body flowed with renewed hope.

"That's good thinking," praised Danny. "However, if Shorty fails to make it, they may cancel the search altogether." He threw the stick into the fire like a spear and walked away.

Standing by the smoke, it seemed ironic to Beth that Shorty's safety meant her rescue. She was starting to enjoy the island but there was a nagging fear that Shorty would come back. A movement out of the corner of her eye caught her attention. She turned to see a large deer's glossy black eyes peering at her. Somehow, she knew that it was the dead deer's mother. Speaking without any emotion, her lips tightened. "I hope he drowns."

Twelve

Taught in the school of hard knocks, Shorty had studied the bullying thesis and passed with honors. Built like a brick shit house, he had taken on anyone at the drop of a hat. Now, however, he felt very tiny and very frail. With the long steering pole secured in place, he dipped the other widened pole at a slow, consistent pace. Thoughts about discarding the waterproof bag and the deer contents passed through his mind. Believing it might act like shark bait, he decided to dispose of it at a more convenient time. Having little else to do but paddle, he attempted to put everything into perspective.

Tossed around from foster home to foster home, he had endured many abusive foster-parents until being brutally raped by his foster-father at age ten. With the courts believing his guardian instead of him, they had sealed his fate by labeling him a troublemaker and ordered him back home. As soon as that court session ended, he had run away and fought dogs for scraps at garbage bins. Stealing had become a way of life. When caught in the act, he had done a lot of time behind bars for petty crimes without having anyone to bail him out. Being a loner, he had learned how to avoid the long arm of the law by fingering others and promising to find employment. At each attempt at trying to make a fresh start, he had packed in various jobs because others seemed to win the work-related arguments. Also, being more interested in the pay instead of the work, he had learned he was going nowhere fast on a starting wage. Eventually, he had run into others who liked his big talk about easy street and formed a small gang.

His group of untrustworthy riffraff had been streetwise, learning their place in society; like him, and he had found a home with them. In their circle, he had learned to be more organized and searched harder for bigger fishes to fry. Together, they had done anything for money without remorse. Greenbacks had been scarce, making them pool together to try to get ahead. As luck would have it, they had spent what little they had as soon as they got it. Eventually, they formalized a golden opportunity. Pooling their savings, they had gotten Shorty on a cruise where the passengers carried lots of gambling cash. Shorty had proved to be in his element by breaking into rooms. Besides robbing money, identification had proven to be a valuable asset. It gave him the information he'd need to eventually rob them at their homes.

Thinking back to the beginning of his petty crimes, he had drawn the line when it involved hurting others. In most cases, however, the ones he helped had stabbed him in the back with some devious falsehood or bum rap. The one person he had thought cared about him turned out to be a cop. Most of the others had ended up as witnesses for the prosecution. Yes, he had learned in the school of hard knocks about helping others. As for the two people stranded on the island, he would look into the possibility of any rewards for their whereabouts. If none were offered, they could rot in hell as far as he was concerned. He had tried to make amends to Beth only to be denounced and turned away.

As time passed, paranoia set in. Would Beth and Danny press charges? No doubt, they'd stick. Even if they never stretched the truth, they had the straight dope on him.

No matter how you sliced it, he had to prevent them from taking the stand. Visions of his huge hairy hands clamping around their puny throats, strangling the life from them, entertained his vengeance to return.

Maybe Danny hadn't given him the correct co-ordinates. If the GPS reading put him on track for China, and with the raft moving as slow as molasses in January, he had a snowball's chance in hell of making it. What a dope, he'd put his trust in complete strangers and pushed forward with the crude shaped oar. Time passed as slowly as a dead snail. He couldn't even sleep. The stress made his mind reel throughout the whole night. With barely any shut-eye, the light of the new morning hurt his eyes.

In the late afternoon, he noticed clouds forming in the distance behind him. He knew little about weather, but he knew this didn't look good. He started paddling with a renewed vigor, like a bat out of hell hyped on adrenaline cocktails, heading for the mainland.

Lightening the load, he threw the animal remains overboard. He could only hope sharks and whales and storms would stay away. Images of being swallowed by a whale and trying to climb out its spout flashed through his mind. With his oar, he pushed the refuse as hard as he could and paddled in the water even harder.

He thought about praying and making promises, but not by any stretch of the imagination could he be believable. For one, he'd have to give up on coming back to the island to cover his tracks. He stopped and pulled the pole back onto the raft for a short rest, watching the bag float some distance behind. Then he studied the sky.

Storm clouds formed and closed fast. Returning to the island now was out of the question as long as a slim chance existed of getting back to the security of his friends. Gale winds of over twenty-five miles per hour began blowing him farther out to sea and peppering his face with salt water.

Swallowed up in blasts of sea spray, the bag with the animal remains gusted around in the raft's currents and now followed closely behind. After a few failed attempts of pushing it away with the longer pole, Shorty decided to submerge it.

Stabbing repeatedly at the plastic bag, he tried to sink it under water. The bloated contents spilled out, floating behind him.

A large wave tossed the deer's head through the air and onto the craft. Some of the other innards landed on Shorty. "Shit!" he said, kicking the small head off and poking it under water. Anxious to distance himself from the animal carcass, he leapt up and down to get a better angle to push it to a greater distance. Feeling his legs separating, he glanced down as the logs began separating. With his heart pounding in his chest, he searched for the vines holding the logs together. They were tied together but stretched like elastic. With the loosening vines beginning to slip off of the butts of the logs, he knelt and reached to lock as many logs as he could into place. At first he used the pole to keep them in check. Then, when the water got rougher, he discarded the paddling device and held as many logs as he could with out-stretched arms. At the peak of each new wave, the deer head reappeared close to his face. Salt water burned Shorty's eyes and nostrils. He felt totally helpless. The fawn's two soft pupils stared quietly into his, being the only witness to his raft's destruction.

Shorty cursed loudly at the animal while wind and rain tore his craft apart. With the GPS unit strung around his neck, he grasped the floatation suitcase and jumped overboard.

As his waist touched the water, he wondered why Danny would want to stay on the island. He must have known Shorty would end up in trouble, but he didn't care. He only wanted to rid himself and his precious Beth from Shorty's presence by sending him on a one way ticket into the unknown. Shorty decided to pay him back. Fortunately, he had observed Danny plug the island coordinates into the GPS and knew they were correct. With revenge on his mind and a new determination, Shorty treaded water and then, like the wind, he headed in the direction of those readings. He was a man on a mission, with a score to settle.

Thirteen

It didn't take long for the downpour to drench both Beth and Danny and to trash the crude shelter. Waiting out the storm, they settled under what was left of the roof.

"Well," said Beth, shaking her head, "so much for our rescue."

"The storm must've caught him with his pants down like it did us," said Danny. "Just because the sun shone, making this island feel like paradise, we took for granted a little hut would do. We forgot about the storm we survived. As well, it was much too early to send Shorty on a raft."

"Poor Shorty," she groaned. She pointed a finger in her mouth as if to throw up. "One day, I'll cry in my beer to remember him, if I ever get a beer."

"I'll buy." Being saved because of the fight over the deer, Danny knew the fickle finger of fate had intervened. No matter how you sliced it, he had been the odds-on-favorite over Beth to travel with Shorty. If Shorty decided against going alone, Danny might've had to travel with him to keep him away from Beth. Another alternative would've had been for Danny to leave the island with her. As it worked out, Shorty had agreed to do the honors. And for that, Danny could thank his lucky stars that he had decided to stay put with Beth.

Inside of twenty-four hours, the storm let up. For the following two days, they worked hard at feeding the signal fires and at rebuilding the crude shelter. By working hard, a large lean-to near the ocean was ready to be turned into a cabin as their reward. Then, they began paying attention to basic amenities.

To construct flexible bed frames, they used vines to tie thin bamboo sticks across a couple of logs. For additional comfort, they trussed together cereal straws and bamboo grasses as mattresses.

Danny worried about the exposure to the wind in this location. He didn't really want to do it all over again after the next storm. "I want to build another house," he said. "A more permanent house that's closer to dry wood, to building timbers, and to fresh water."

"You mean, for you?" asked Beth. She stopped weaving a bamboo grass mattress. "This is it. You want to move."

"No, no," explained Danny. "You got it all wrong. We have to build somewhere safer. I liked the idea of a tree house overlooking the lake, but it might rip apart in wind. I believe a one-story shack would be more practical. What do you think?"

"We got lots of time," she said. "We could really build something nice."

"Yes," he said. The idea of carving beauty into existing beauty hit home as ideas began to formulate in his thoughts. 'I'll bet we can."

"I'd like to live by the lake," she said.

"Living by the edge of the freshwater lake would free up the water jugs," he said. His mouth watered at the thought of making and storing fruit juices. "As well, the lake provides protection for the front part of the shack while an opening at the rear would grant a view of the interior of the island."

"Wow!" she said. "I have a feeling it's going to look nice."

His mind raced at the possibilities until one place beat all the others. To the left of this new location, a narrow, stream sprang out of a large mound and surged inside a deep ditch to feed the lake. On the right, a creek flowed on a gentle slope out of the lake and fed the ocean. Here, smack dab in the middle, some giant coconut trees provided a framework for even a possible skyscraper let alone a one-story hut. The outer areas teemed with various fruit trees and berry bushes and Danny pointed at them. "Weeding and pruning would allow neatness and visibility.

Beth smiled. "They could be transplanted to form perfect hedges."

"Wading through their thickness, any wild animals would make a lot of noise and warn us," added Danny. "On the other hand, the distance from the ocean prevents us from checking for signs of rescue. With any luck, the unattended signal fires will do the work."

Danny kept Beth up to date on all plans, trying to make her feel as though she were in good hands. The more he told her right away, the less he'd have to explain later. He hoped she'd find some kind of hobby. For him, the interesting geology hidden in the island kept him intrigued.

Lots of glassy obsidian rock lay scattered throughout the island. He smashed a large chunk on a larger stone, smiling as it broke into many shiny slabs. Sorting them in order of size, he believed the pieces could function as sharp-edged tools. With one of the larger ones, he began cutting the brush between the four large trees. While he worked, Beth hauled the waste to a nearby fire pit. He smiled again. She was becoming more independent, which was important because he didn't have time to point out every little chore that needed doing.

In one day they gathered a sizable quantity of bamboo poles. Making their efforts pay off, they using vines and logs for framework for the ceiling and the floor. After forming a couple of rough beds on those floor logs, they settled in for the night.

~ * ~

Danny woke early. Except for the sound of waves hitting the shores and for some birds in the distance making a lot of noise the island was quiet. Putting it aside, he started working diligently completing the wood structure of the roof by putting the bamboo poles in place.

Beth began tying them together. Just before the sun set directly overhead she broke the silence and the pace. "Something isn't right. Birds are loud."

"Yeah," he agreed. "We better keep on our toes. When I'm prospecting alone in the bush in Canada, the birds really get loud when a bear is in the same area. I think it's instinctive for birds to warn or to call out when something interesting is happening."

As her head craned towards Danny, he noticed that her second chin jiggled uncontrollably. Although her open mouth failed to find the words, yet her gaping eyes said how much she worried.

"Something may be setting up a kill," he stated flatly to make it sound like nothing. "It's likely some deer near here."

"Far away," her voice squeaked.

"It sounds close by," he whispered. "It could be a jaguar or a wolf."

Glancing from tree to tree, as though trying to pinpoint the direction of the noise, she turned her back to Danny.

He chuckled to himself, thinking about grasping her from behind to scare the daylights out of her. If she were anyone else, he may have done it to break the monotony and to strike up some laughter. Watching her big arse brake to a halt each time she turned seemed to be funny enough. Quietly, he went back to work.

Fourteen

Beth's spine tingled. She was alone in the camp but felt as though her every movement was being watched. When Danny appeared, the feeling left. "Were you out there looking at me?"

"What do you mean?" He paused and looked at his feet.

"I mean, it felt real creepy," she explained. "I could feel someone watching me and you showed up. Were you out there?" Standing right in front of him, she wondered why he wouldn't look her in the eyes.

"Not me," he claimed. Waving her away, he turned to walk away. Over his shoulder he commented, "Sometimes I wonder if I'm better off being alone."

"Guess its true," she replied. "Only the animals like me."

"Listen up, I'm sick of you trying to play on my heart strings." Danny turned toward her. He pointed a finger in her face. "You talk about no one seeing your inner beauty. Well, guess what? Look in a mirror and see the one who hates you the most. When you learn to like yourself, try working harder to get others to like you. Otherwise, keep your inner beauty comments to yourself."

"Say what?" she mumbled. As she didn't want him to repeat everything, the words came out of her mouth in a reflex to what he said. He seemed unusually mean today. Staring straight ahead, she got the impression that he wanted to get rid of her. By getting upset with her, it would be a lot easier for him to live with himself if he planned to do her in.

"You heard me. As for someone watching you, maybe we invaded some wild animal's territory. Maybe they're not all your friends."

At that comment, sarcastic or not, Beth spent a lot of time listening to the forest. To fill her time, she utilized small vines and began weaving a blanket. Feeling soft to the skin, the vines made an excellent choice for materials. Regardless of the warm nights, lots of blankets for mattresses, for chairs, and for decorations would be nice. Various shades of greens and browns allowed many patterns.

She stopped what she was doing as a movement caught her eye. It was Danny leaving by the eastern side of camp. He seemed changed somehow. Was it for the better?

After twenty minutes she heard the forest to the west quiet. Beginning to knit faster, her nervous fingers raced her thumping heart. Everything seemed amplified. Her shaking became uncontrollable. Trying to stay calm, she glanced repeatedly toward the bushes. Lying next to her, a sharp, layered obsidian stone appeared to be larger than before. In a cunning sudden movement, she moved the stone closer. She could taste someone or something near. Next time, she concluded, she would stay near Danny if possible.

Within three hours, Danny arrived back. "Look at these," he said happily. His cupped hands contained some small potatoes. While handing them to her, his eyeballs roamed over the length of the cover she had sewn. "Geese, that's something."

"It's going to be a blanket." Noticing for the first time how long it would turn out to be when completed, she blushed. The forest noises seemed natural now. She put that to the back of her mind. She added, "For a bed."

"Looks like it could cover both beds at the same time."

The sharp words cut into her. She stammered, "Well...Well, queen size."

"Giant-size is more accurate." His nostrils inhaled deeply, making an obvious display of sarcasm.

"We can use it as a rug."

"It could make either a roof or a house."

She changed the subject. "Where did you find those?"

"A whole football field of them just to the..." he hesitated, "...northeast. They're a small potato, but in large numbers." His glance adverted from the northeast to the west and than to the blanket. "Maybe you could fold that into a mattress."

"Yeah," she nodded woodenly. "Whatever you think."

"Pretty quiet around camp, huh?"

She trembled. Was there a hidden meaning to that question? Chills crept up her spine. But at least he was giving her the time of day, and for that she was glad. Yet, she shrank away, still wondering why he asked.

Danny started washing the potatoes.

Keeping him within shouting distance, she slipped off towards the part of the forest that gripped her attention earlier.

~ * ~

Her eyes scanned the area. Funny how the terrain felt friendly now that she knew she wasn't alone. Checking behind some bushes, she found an area with some fresh human tracks. Knowing better, she wanted to believe someone else had been spying on the camp. Thinking they might be old tracks, she decided to follow them. The footprints led her to a freshly dug hole, which resembled a shallow, wide gravesite. Gasping for breath, she darted towards camp.

She realized just how little she knew her island mate. Teardrops edged down her cheeks. Soon, two weak wobbly knees lost stability. Collapsing on the ground, she gasped for air. Along with her breath, she also seemed to lose her reasoning.

The two ancient gravesites contained treasure beyond imagination, and that Danny had already dug them up. That had to be the reason for his odd behavior. It would've also been a good reason for Danny to sent Shorty off alone too. But as evil as Shorty was, she needed him now. At least he fought for his life, rather than for money. She hoped that she could convince Danny that he could have it all. She wanted to live.

She shook violently. Did Danny know that she knew what he was up to?

Tear stained and exhausted, she staggered through the clearing, within sight of Danny, to the lake. Ducking her head under water, she cried and hoped the fish would hear her story. Gasping for air at each bob, she remained there for about an hour. Facing facts, she pulled herself together. Strutting toward camp, she felt ready to do battle. It was time to put him in his place by making the first move.

~ * ~

"It's time to build another boat. I can use the sun, stars and my watch for direction. It's almost as good as a compass." Glassy eyes searched for Beth's approval.

She squinted and tried to pierce his hard exterior for some sort of read. She was certain he wouldn't need her after the boat was built. "Sure, you bet your boots." She turned away and spoke over her shoulder. "I'll get on the menial work right away. Anything you find too tedious you just let me know."

After his head jerked back, his eyes opened wider "What?"

"You throw your weight around like nobody's business. Do I even exist in your world?"

He gaped at her.

"Ha!" she exclaimed, reading guilt in his reaction. "You make me sick." The rhythm of her heart kicked up a notch, positive he was hiding something. She thought about helping and then trying to escape afterward, but her pride kicked in. "Actually, you do what you want, and I'll do what I want."

Looking as if his jaw would've hit the ground if not for his stretched cheeks, Danny stepped back. The gaping mouth searched for words. "What?"

"What!" Stomping her feet in a fury, Beth stormed away. "Are you deaf?" Looking back, she shouted, "Piss off! Touch me and I'll kill you!"

Working alone, the beat red fellow set about building the raft.

Fifteen

Even if her mood appeared to be change with the wind, Danny blamed himself for being so mean to Beth. In all the time they spent together, he had mentioned little about his ex-wife and even less about himself. He knew that he had to get his act together and make her feel welcome. For now, he put her out of his mind and concentrated on the task at hand.

As a ten-foot wide craft would have enough space to maneuver down the small creek, he decided to build a boat on the calm lake at the mouth of the creek well away from the hut. The still water would make it easier to work on. To help make the craft seaworthy, he soaked the vines for a couple days to prevent any unexpected stretching later. Something he'd overlooked on the first raft. While the vines soaked in the lake, he gathered logs.

When he worked on the boat, Beth worked on the house. Whenever he went to help with the house, she left to gather more bamboo. When he searched for logs, she would stare in the bush as though trying to determine his whereabouts. At night she stayed awake, sitting beside the fire. Danny tried to cheer her up, but she would sneer and distance herself. Getting the point, he thought it better to leave her alone.

With bloodshot eyeballs, she began the next day. It went much the same as the previous day. By evening, all four walls of the shack were completed. Sleeping alone in the new home, Beth's snoring and sobbing probably carried as far as the mainland. Worried for her, instead of sleeping by the fire, he camped by her door.

After waking, he searched for coconuts for the journey. With the raft nearing completion, he needed a break and went to the fire pit.

Staying out of his sight, she circled around to the freshly dug gravesite. Lots of new footprints covered the site. A rabbit's ear and fur pieces littered the bottom of the hole. Through gritting teeth, she muttered, "Bastard!"

Picking up a long sharp stick, she jabbed it in the air at an invisible enemy repeatedly. Soon, she lay on the sand, gasping and sobbing. When the crying stopped, she stormed towards camp and waved the stick over her head.

At the campsite, Danny sat on a log. Pinching both nostrils tight, he drew in a large breath and held it until the feeling of the sneeze passed. He knew that this was a dangerous way of suppressing a cough. Sleeping the night away from the fire, he had picked up a slight cold. Now, it seemed to be reaching a new peak. Blowing his runny nose, he glanced at the clear skies wondering how a cold could survive. As most violent ones do, this one seemed as though it would last forever. Out of the corner of his eye, he noticed Beth stomping into the clearing to his far left. She looked rundown and seemed to be talking to herself. He fixed his stare into the sky.

Glancing at him, she darted past him and into the hut. With the stick in her grasp, she closed the bamboo and vine door.

Within an hour, his curiosity got the best of him. In stealth mode, he skirted around to the brush line and towards the shack. Nearing, he could hear crying and muttering in prayer. Perhaps, he reasoned, if he could make out what she was saying, he could get to the bottom of this insanity.

"How could it come to this?" she rambled, barely audible. "I didn't demand much out of life. Everything I got I either inherited or was given to me. I've never had to do anything on my own. Now, I have to deal with him." He could hear the cracking of wood, believing it was from her squeezing the wood stick. Soon, the sobs took control. He heard her drop on the sand, on all fours, before wailing like an ear-shattering siren that started and stopped repeatedly.

Stunned, Danny stepped back. He got the impression she wanted to help more. Perhaps a few more compliments for her efforts had been in order. She deserved better. There had to be ways to make the distraught woman feel better. Feeling a cough coming on, he stepped back and pinched his nose.

He heard the stick's swooshing and jabbing sounds. "Die," she screamed. "Die! Die!"

The new sounds made him more concerned. Holding his nose and breath, he crawled through some tall grass. Slowly releasing his breath, he tiptoed along the side of the cabin until reaching an opening in the structure resembling a window. Without warning, he coughed.

At the sound, she leapt up.

After controlling the cough, he peaked in the window.

"Bastard," she cried! Tears streamed down her large, red cheeks from gaping, bloodshot eyeballs.

He'd only seen actors in movies before give such a frightened look. He wanted to shout how sorry he felt, but all he could do was stand with his mouth hanging open. The hand holding the spear moved quickly and he jumped back.

The spear hurtled through the opening. Missing him by mere fractions of a millimeter, he stepped backward.

Pick ing up a coconut, she darted out the front door to the back of the building. Comparable to a winning World

Series' pitch, she pitched the dry coconut.

The large nut bounced off his head.

He fell forward as stars danced in front of his eyes. He faded in and out of consciousness for what felt like a hundred times before his nose touched the sand. He reached up to rub the intense pain in his forehead but found his hand paralyzed. He couldn't move. He could only get his green eyes to move in their sockets. She picked up another coconut from a pile and for the life of him, he could have sworn he spoke, but the words didn't come. He hoped to convey his message with pleading eyes.

Winding up, she threw for another strike.

In shock, his glazed eyes grew as the sphere neared. The projectile ricocheted from the back of his head, bouncing straight up before falling. He finally found his strength and leapt to his feet. His wobbly legs made a run for it.

Turning, she reached for another coconut.

Scrambling through vegetation, he glanced backward. Seeing the new missile in her grasp, he covered the back of his head with one hand while the other cleared a flight path through for his body.

"Try that shit on me again and you'll really get what for." Retrieving the spear, she retreated inside the cabin.

Bruised and beaten, he had no idea what she thought he was doing at the window. Resisting the urge to go back and ask her, he decided to return to the boat.

Staying away from the hut that night, he set out to sleep on the boat's log bottom. During the windless night, he thought he heard the brushes moving. Remaining alert, he imagined her moving around in the darkness.

Sixteen

Beth was convinced that Danny would try something in the night. Something stirred in the brush, but her tired and worn out body shivered and remained in place. Before long, she passed out from fatigue.

Something touched her dress by her stomach and woke her. She squeezing her eyelids shut and feigned sleep. It felt like a hand. She wished it were that giant toad. Whatever it was, it inched towards her dress opening and onto her thigh. Anticipating its next move, she felt the hairy fingers reaching for her exposed privates.

Confirming a light, hairy touch, her mind screamed as she narrowed the possibilities. Her eyeballs popped her eyelids open and glanced down. She screamed! When she finally came to her senses, she clenched her teeth and made an effort to remain as still as possible.

Shaking violently, she waited for a bite of a different nature. Horrified, she watched the large tarantula-like spider crawl ever so slowly up her thigh. When it finally moved onto the sandy floor, Beth sprang upright and searched the room for others. In the dim night's light, she saw a wide gap in the wall where the spider must have come from. Someone had pried apart some tall bamboo. Had the spider been corralled there purposely? Beth could hear footsteps pounding on the sand closing in on the hut, and she hid in the shadows.

Danny charged in, kicking the door into pieces. Poised in a boxer's stance, he danced around the room. He neared the back wall and Beth charged for the doorway.

"You're a son-of-a-bitch!" Flitting out of the opening, she pointed the sharp stick at him in warning. She added, "Just because I'm alone!"

He took one look, obviously deciding to give up the fight and exited the door as quickly as he'd entered.

She pulled herself together and scurried to the raft. Checking back, she hoped she had a good lead but noticed Danny closing fast.

He shouted, "Please stop!"

"Piss off!" Hurling her sharp stick at him, she warned, "Stay back!" Pushing the raft free, she searched for an intimidating weapon. Off and running, she boarded. Grabbing the long pole, she stabbed first at him then at the water. Furiously, she pushed at the sandy bottom. The raft began to move out into the lake.

Standing at the shoreline, he waved his arms overhead. "Come back."

"Stay away!" She swore, "I'll kill you!" With the vine and rock anchor cast overboard, she stopped forty meters off shore. Swinging the long pole menacingly around, she bellowed, "I've had enough! Try something and you'll get yours!"

He shook his head and returned in the direction of the shack. "You're crazy. I hope the boat sinks!"

Lying on the makeshift bed on the open boat, she cried herself to sleep.

~ * ~

After gathering firewood for the camp and other such chores, he waved to her and set out in the direction of the signal fires.

Seeing him leave, she hoisted anchor and set a bearing for the hut. She labored; paddling until the pole touched the sandy bottom. Beginning at the bow, she pushed the long pole aft until she ended up at the stern. After docking the craft by beaching it, she jumped onto the sand.

A couple hundred feet inland, she found some chokecherry bushes but as she picked she felt as though someone was watching her. Shivering, she dashed towards the houseboat with some berries cupped in the folds of the cloth of the short dress. The safety of the raft, well in the water, seemed her best bet. "Damn you!" she yelled. The berries fell to the ground. Tears formed in her eyes, blocking her view of the boat.

The houseboat floated about thirty feet off shore, in four separate pieces. Its vines drifted beside the logs and appeared untied. They couldn't have had come undone by themselves in still water, she concluded. There must be a reason. Her mind worked feverishly to pick holes in Danny's offensive tactics.

What would she do now? Why hide and flee? Sooner or later, she would get caught. Would the pain and terror be worth it? No, facing him was what she had to do.

Finding another large sharp stick, she stood in the doorway of the shack to wait for him.

It didn't take long before Danny strutted into the campsite, dragging some thin vines behind him. "Hey Beth," he called out. "What happened to the boat?"

"Oh it fell apart," she answered as friendly as she could. What sort of sick thing had he planned next, she wondered? Squeezing both eyelids tight, she shut out visions of being tied up and left to starve. "Come any closer," she warned, "and you'll get yours."

His eyebrows tightened before vanishing in his hairline. He didn't say a word.

Not that she would expect him to. He was up to

something. That much she knew. She just didn't know what. "Want to break things," she shouted. "She began punching at the walls."

With eyes trained on the raft, he pressed on towards it.

Taking a break to rest her bloody knuckles, she watched him throughout the day. While one nostril remained plugged, the unplugged nostril blew long, loud exhales while she frothed at the mouth.

His fingers worked slowly and meticulously. Besides retrieving all parts of the raft, he used twice as many vines as before tied together with all sorts of knots to ensure it stayed together. Then, he headed toward Beth.

She blocked the doorway into the shack and pointed the sharp end of her spear at him. "Stay back!"

"Please, can I get my suitcases?"

"Wait there!" After disappearing into the building, she placed two suitcases outside the door and went back inside. She warned, "Don't you dare make a false move!"

With the two cases in hand, he climbed aboard the raft.

When he reached the middle of the lake, she tasted confusion. What was he waiting for? She sat at the doorway watching the raft until three AM. With sleep threatening, she tied the repaired bamboo poled door shut and curled up in a corner. She snored, out to the world, resting on a lifejacket.

She woke in a coughing fit. Heavy smoke burned her nostrils and filled the hut while flames licked up each side. Screaming, she leapt erect. Holding the lifejacket, she reached her hands forward to find the wall. Using her head, she butted her way outside.

The raft came to shore.

Sitting on the sand, she touched the newly forming lumps on her head and started to cry.

Emerging out of the water, Danny ran to the burning hut. "What the hell happened?"

"Please, stay away." She sobbed. "I've had enough."

He stared at her briefly. "It's just an accident, I guess." Turning to the blaze, he started pulling the shack apart with his bare hands and kicked sand on the fire. Every now and then he stopped to pat the heat from his hands. "Why are you doing all those crazy things?" He shouted at her. "What is wrong with you?"

"Keep away!" Brushing back her light brown hair, she cringed at the growing swellings on her head. She didn't think the hut's walls were so sturdy, but they were enough to cause considerable pain. She got to her feet and strapped on the lifejacket. Stomping to the water, she turned towards him. "Go away. I'll bite your head off if you come near."

He stared after her, but stopped. Instead, he kept pulling at logs and smothering the flames.

Slapping hard at the water, she reached the raft and climbed aboard. Hoisting anchor, she paddled the raft further offshore. Nothing could reach her here. Feeling safe and smug, she dropped the rock anchor. Over the clear lake, she could see that the fire was out, and that the white shoreline was black.

~ * ~

Danny sat on the beach while the remains of the hut smoldered. His shoulders drooped in defeat. The small house had taken so long to construct. He stared blindly out over the water until his eyelids closed and his snores echoed in the night.

The following day, while he set about constructing a lean-to, Beth stayed on the raft and Danny had no desire to coax her inland. The lean-to was small; after constructing the bed, he crawled in. He figured she'd come ashore when she thought she was safe from whatever danger he presented. She was going mad, and if she stayed away, that was just fine with him too.

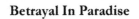

Seventeen

Through the night, Beth struggled with the low river bottom. Aching for rest, her tired body craved food. The sun's radiant rays appeared on the horizon. Her bloodshot eyes observed the brilliant reflections on the less than hundred feet of clear water, which separated the raft from the deep salty green ocean waters. Knowing freedom sat a stone's throw, she worked up a second wind.

Sounds broke behind her in the brush.

Tiredness was secondary. The long pole stabbed at the sandy bottom with renewed pace. The raft picked up speed. When it grounded on a sandbank, she almost fell off because of the momentum. Leaping into the water, her straining muscles began pushing the craft.

"Beth," called the sharp voice. "Where are you?" Danny was following the riverbank. "Come back!" he bellowed. "You need me!"

She shook her head in case she hadn't heard him clearly. What could she possibly need him for? She jumped in the water and over the embankment. Scrambling through some brush, she headed blindly in a direction away from his voice.

She dashed headlong into open arms. She screamed and her heart stopped. In the terrifying silence, she looked up at her captor. Dazed until her ticker began ticking, she regained her balance. "Shorty!" she cried. "I'm glad to see you!"

"Uh--"

"Danny's gone mad," she explained between breaths. "He wants the treasure for himself."

Loosening his grip on her, he stepped back. His brows shot up. "Oh?"

"Yeah!" she confirmed. "It's in the graves. The graves are loaded with treasure." Her chest heaved as she struggled to catch her breath.

"Do you know where they are?" His fingers tightened around her arms. He pushed his large jaw forward, touching her upper lip. "Quickly, tell me now!"

She tasted his ugly breath and felt his piercing eyes. She was more confused than ever. Maybe it was best to remain quiet about the gravesites. Pushing at his chest, she stepped back. "Where did you come from?"

"I…" stammered Shorty. "I just got here."

She swept her eyes over his dry clothes. "How--"

"Danny set a trap for me too," interjected Shorty quickly. "He must have known about that treasure earlier."

"I believe that."

Sounds came out of the brush behind Beth.

As if handling a work of art, Shorty asked point blank, "Do you know where the treasure is?"

Nodding acknowledgement, she turned towards the oncoming sounds.

Shorty stepped away. "Don't worry," he said sharply. "I'll take care of him.

She knew she faced an important decision so she worked hard to recall similar situations from the TV soaps. Now she knew why she had spent so much time watching them. It was for this moment. Life would be easier if Danny could be restrained. Her mind clicked. Her finger pointed. "Hide in the bush."

Gripping a large hardwood club, Shorty hid.

Eighteen

Sighting the raft, Danny leapt into the water to inspect it. His hands pushed and pulled, convincing him it was in good shape. Noticing it sat on a sandbank, he pictured Beth polling the raft until it grounded and abandoning it rather than getting into the water to push it free. How unusual, but how her.

"Danny," she called, stepping into a clearing.

He turned with a questioning look in response.

Remaining silent, she stood still.

He walked towards her. There had to be something he could do to set her mind at ease. Up close, however, anger took over. "What do you think you're doing?" he asked harshly. "Are you going out to sea by yourself? Is your brain in your buttocks?"

"I know you want to finish me off," she said. "You must be ashamed! I'm only a woman." She glanced at Shorty for approval.

Shorty remained hidden, gripping a large hardwood club and smiling encouragingly.

Danny stopped. As though trying to say he didn't understand, he raised and spread his hands apart ever so slightly. "You're off your rocker." He was irritated now. "I'll bet you have to exert yourself to think of someone who misses you."

"Know-it-all!" she shouted curtly. "Here I am!"

He sighed. "I'm sorry for saying that. Don't sweat it, the raft is fine."

"Come on you creep!" she shouted. She was trying to egg him on, trying to pick a fight but for what reason was beyond Danny. "You don't know your ass from a hole in the ground. I'm tired of your shit! Get it over with!"

He was too tired to argue. "What's the matter with you, huh?" He turned around and headed toward the raft, with his finger waving in a circle at his temple. Yep, she was nuts.

"Wait," she called after him. "You wrecked the other boat and sent a spider to get me. When that failed, you burned the shack down." Picking a stone off the sandy ground, she hurled it at Danny.

Missing by a few feet, the projectile thudded into the sand.

Glancing down, Danny recognized a large piece of sharp biotite. "You're crazy." He turned towards her. "Where did you get such a stupid idea? Lady, it's time to rethink whatever it is you've got going on inside that thing you call a brain because you're dead wrong."

"Cut the crap!" With her left arm extended, she curled her fingers back and forth, inviting him onward. She held her right fist by her face. "Here I am!"

"Why would I do all those things you said I did?" His blood pressure must be rising, and he knew he should calm down. Taking a large breath, he gritted his teeth and glared at her. "All it did was made me more work."

"You almost got rid of me," she continued. "Big Foot, you scare me all to hell!" Picking up a sharp stick, she pitched it at his feet. "Here! Use this. The treasure will be all yours."

"What kind of person do you take me for?" Danny's brows shot up and his eyes opened wide. He shook his head and stared at her in utter disbelief. "After all I did for you. I saved your life."

"Now I'm here," she said, sounding disgusted. She dropped to her knees on the soft sand. "I'm ripe for the picking."

"What?"

"Here I am, easy picking."

Danny shook his head. "I'm a non-violent person."

She stretched her hand. "Well, either choke me or help me up."

"You're crazy." He moved to take her hand. "You know I wouldn't do anything to hurt you."

"If it wasn't you, then who was it?"

Danny followed her nervous, averted glance. Movement behind some logs and a flowery plant made him jump back. He lifted his arm to protect his head.

As the club connected, the crunching of crushed bone echoed across the island.

Holding his elbow, Danny fell to the ground.

Shouting to stop, Beth leapt in Shorty's path. "It was you! Not Danny!"

Sidestepping, he shoved her behind him. His other hand swung the giant stick towards Danny's head.

Turning sideways, the club walloped Danny's shoulder instead. Pain swept to the break in the same arm. He rolled to avoid more strikes. He knew he must try to get up to be less of a target. He was an easy mark lying on the ground. Through a haze of pain, he glanced up. Shorty held the weapon held high above his head, ready to deliver the final flow. Danny twisted away.

He blinked twice and forced himself to sit up in time to see Shorty teeter and fall face first to the ground. His body convulsed in the sand beside Danny. Beth had knocked Shorty out. He held his arm and looked at her in confusion.

She held a large coconut over her head. "Go!" she

commanded. "Go now, before I change my mind."

Danny slowly got to his feet. He knew that while prospecting in South America he could encounter many adventures. Bandits, local farmers, kidnappers and such, he could understand, but this? How could he put up with the craziness? He'd much rather be alone in the wilds. Here, things moved faster than he could comprehend. "I never thought you'd be insane and pair up with Shorty."

Shorty stirred and reached out.

With his good hand, Danny grasped Shorty's ankle and wedged it about four inches off the ground. Then he leapt down, landing his knee on Shorty's, twisting up at the same time.

With a snapping sound, Shorty's knee broke. Falling on top the leg, Danny twisted it further. He disjointed the knee even more by rotating it as far as it would go.

Waving the coconut high in the air, Beth screamed, "Stop Danny! Enough! You'll kill him!" Then she lunged.

Jumping backward, Danny held up his good hand, "Please stop. Please."

Falling, both her body and the nut fell short and landed on Shorty.

Grimacing loudly, Shorty came to and swung his fist at her.

Beth countered by striking the nut on his nose.

As dark red blood gushed from his nose, Shorty fell back and lost consciousness.

She struck him a few more times and then turned toward Danny.

"What the hell is going on?" demanded Danny. He found his feet and stood above her. Frustration ran rampant in his blood and he wanted some answers. How long had Shorty been here, and what was he after?

"How long have you two been working together?"

"Stay back," she warned.

Holding his own injured arm, he stepped back and re-thought the recent events. He nodded his head as understanding dawned. "It's all pretty clear," he began. Perhaps he could trick her into filling in the gaps. "I'll bet you dollars to donuts you just ran into him a few minutes ago. Otherwise, with his help, you would've gotten the boat to the ocean. I assume he was shipwrecked in the storm and swam back. Then, with your help, he intended to murder me. But with me out of the way, he still had one key witness to attempted murder."

She stared at him while teardrops overflowed her lower lids and flowed down her cheeks. She nodded. "I promised him treasure." With eyes averted, she got to her feet.

"That's something to tell him." Danny shook his head in disbelief. "I hope you're happy."

Beth pointed her watery eyes toward the ground.

Each movement was a new experience in pain, but Danny made his way to the raft. On the day he had completed the craft, he had stowed all his equipment on board. As Beth's had burned in the fire, he was glad that he had stashed it separately. Finding elastic bandages and metal fasteners, he gathered a few, dried bamboo sticks. He winced as pain bit through his arm at each wrap of his crude splint. When completed the wrapping, his good arm tied his fractured arm against his chest with a long soft vine. He glared at Shorty. "Let's see what he has to say."

Shorty lay on the ground, gaping at his leg's awkward position in relation to his body. Tears streamed down his face as he glared at Danny. "I thought that Danny knew the storm was coming, and that the raft would sink because the vines stretched."

Danny sighed. He could only imagine the hell Shorty must have went through at sea. "Do you want me to try to pop your knee into place?"

In obvious pain, he shook his head. "Thanks, but I'm hurting enough. You're no doctor. I could live with the pain. I'll be good from now on."

"It sounds like leaving the island at any time soon is dangerous." Danny looked at the burly man and then at the surroundings. "Even if you sound sincere," Danny warned and peered into Shorty's eyes, "you'd better stay on that side of the island. The far river is our divider until I build a fence. You live on the south half of the island where the accommodations had been built earlier. I understand the trouble you had at sea, but killing me in cold blood tells me something."

Danny turned toward Beth. "And *you* went off the deep end. Maybe it's my fault, maybe it's not. But if you want, I'll build you a houseboat."

Nineteen

Beth put her heart into it, giving Danny's injured body a helping hand to push the raft back to the lake for her to live on. Within a week, Danny and Beth completed another raft and docked it near hers. To settle any unforeseen land disputes with Shorty about fence crossings, Danny started constructing a crude wood gate to allow Shorty access to a small portion of a stream and a small stretch of the lake's beach.

Usually, Shorty kept out of Beth's sight. Once, his fire went out. He used a crutch to walk into Danny's work area. Danny gave him a burning log, and Shorty returned the GPS unit.

The sight of the hobbling man put Beth's mind at ease. Only a small threat remained of the large man, and that one swift kick in his leg area would take care of him. After living a few months on the water, she learned that the raft's location made it hard for any predators like him to reach her.

~ * ~

Beth stepped out of the raft's lean-to and stretched her half-asleep arms into the rising sun. The fresh air filled her lungs, pushing her breasts forward. The sun had tightened and darkened her skin. She had lost a lot of weight with her daily swims to shore and her new physical life. Everything about her took a larger than life turn, only comparable to a wonderful dream. Noticing Danny on shore, she dove cleanly into the cool water. With each fine over-stroke, she felt proud and wonderful at her swimming ability and reached the shoreline in hardly any time at all.

On shore, she sat on a log and stretched out both legs. The warming sun penetrated the short tattered dress, sunning and drying her skin. The tears had been stitched with strong thin strands of seaweed to stay together in the water. A fact she had mentioned to Danny about a method for tying the raft's logs together.

Footsteps in the sand made her raise her face. She shielded her eyes with a hand and smiled at Danny. "Hi, Beth," he said. "I'm going out to the fence. Would you like to come along?"

She gazed in the fence's direction and nodded. "It's too bad we have to have such a thing as a fence."

"Well, the extra work and my moving around seem to help my injuries." He nodded. "Besides, we got to keep the animals out." As he walked, he patted a sharp stick in his makeshift scabbard and vine belt.

"Yeah," she agreed, flexing her arm muscles to display her strengths. "Now, it's a simple matter of plundering and burying the booty."

"We each keep separate halves of the map," added Danny.

The fence was a testament to all of Danny's hard work. It had taken a while to construct the log and vine divider but the purpose became twofold. Not only did it keep Shorty away, but also kept the animals on their side safe.

"Look," Danny pointed. "Shorty's fire is still burning."

"Yes," she replied, "good for him." Rather than keep their fires going, Beth had accepted that they are stuck here. They stacked signal fire pits with dry wood in case they had to light them with Danny's few remaining matches. "He's probably trying to recruit someone to help get the treasure. Hope it doesn't attract more like him."

She also realized that Danny had stuck to his strict vegetarian diet, so he could hardly be the one who had left the meat at the gravesite that she discovered earlier. Yet, because Danny had hardly spoken to her, she felt she had a reason to remain cautious earlier on. But now, she knew she would have to live with the fact he liked keeping to himself.

Instead of fence posts, he had used existing single standing trees or had tied three cut trees together with vines to resemble a tripod. The long thin trees he set in them still had branches, reminding her of wire. Arriving at the spot where the work ended the day before, and among the wood shavings spread out on the grass, she noticed the couple of dark slabs of rock used for trimming and falling. She wished she had a canvass and some paint. "Danny," she breathed, "It's so beautiful."

"It's built to last and keep the animals in," he said proudly. He picked up the butt of a tree lying on the ground and worked it close to the fence.

While he constructed, Beth took in the area. Fruit growing nearby caught her attention and she carried a few bananas and pineapples to him. "You better eat if you work."

"I suppose," he said with a nod. After cutting the pineapple with a slice of biotite rock, he sat the slices on some wood shavings. Choosing the largest piece, he sat down on the small log he had ready to put into place.

She set the bananas beside him and headed away into the bushes, choosing to eat while searching for deadwood.

Finding stands of dead trees proved to be easy enough. After pulling each dried out piece of wood from the ground, she dragged it to the fence. Wanting to impress Danny, she took her time and did a good job. For dinner, she found a couple of coconuts and some raspberries. At the end of the day, her shrunken, sweat-saturated dress pulled tight against her skin.

~ * ~

At the lake, the water felt cool and cleansing. Swimming to her raft, she climbed aboard and lay on the logs to dry. Through trial and error, she had learned that the sooner she got back to the raft, the more chance her clothes had of getting perfectly dry. Long before night fell, her tired body fell soundly asleep.

Within four more months they completed the fence. Danny began doing magnetic surveys. To help out, Beth gathered food and did odd jobs.

They sat in the shade of their first hut built by the lake. Beth had helped Danny clean up the burnt wood and had helped rebuilt it so Danny could stay there while building the second raft. "You did pretty good here," complimented Danny. "It might be worth it to fix it up as a house we could relax in during the day or during a storm. Do you feel up to putting a lot of work into it?"

Something behind them distracted her, and she turned toward the noise.

Shorty limped slowly into their camp, using a large hardwood staff as a cane. His free left hand cupped something wrapped up in a huge palm leaf.

Getting to his feet, Danny waited. The aversion on his face said it all.

Remaining seated, Beth curled her nose. "Ugh. Can you smell that?"

"Smoked fish," affirmed Danny.

"Hello," hollered Shorty. He held the leaf package high into the air. "It's for you."

Beth's eyes met Danny's. Then each rolled their eyes.

"What is it?" asked Danny. "What's the occasion?"

"A present of goodwill," he replied, working his way closer. "It's been such a long time since I've seen you guys."

Beth tried to think of proclaiming that date a possible holiday. Thinking that Shorty might take it as an invitation to visit once a year, she abandoned that thought. Besides, the Christmas holiday started in a couple of weeks. It softened her attitude toward Shorty. Danny remained silent; so, she did too, while Shorty hobbled closer. When he got to the edge of the cabin's shade, she saw that he still looked powerful, and that he now sported a beard.

Danny pointed to a log, and Shorty nodded thankfully.

As he stepped over the shade's border, Beth felt helplessly drained. She wanted to leap into the air and scream at him to screw off but she remained quiet. Her burning eyes searched for clues or giveaways by watching, watching, and watching.

Shorty set the fish on the sand.

"Hold it," Danny said curtly. "Keep your dead fish."

Shorty shrugged and drew the leaf package on to his good thigh. He smiled. "Lots of wild animals and strange insects around the island, huh?"

"Are lots of animals hanging around your camp?" Danny asked.

"Yeah, sure thing," replied Shorty. "There are lots of them."

"Probably curious about your kills," said Danny.

"Yeppers," Beth sneered. Thoughts of all the meat she used to eat came to mind. As her stomach turned, she crinkled her nose. "Why don't you share your food with them?"

"Yeah, with a wolf pack," Danny joked.

Shorty's lips tightened. Beth braced herself in case Shorty leapt up and started swinging his club. When his face awkwardly contorted, both lips seemed to touch both ears. It was a phony smile. She said, "Even the birds smell the kill on you and chirp like crazy when you walk around."

Snorting loudly, Danny's eyes narrowed.

"Lucky for all I've a bum leg," threatened Shorty. "You wouldn't talk like that."

"Well, you are," retorted Beth. "And we do. Now take your dead fish over to your side of the island before I kick your ass myself."

"It's too bad you never got it earlier," Shorty grunted. Breathing heavily, he glared at them.

Pointing south, Danny lowered his voice. "Listen," he said, with all pretense of friendliness gone. "You better leave camp right now. And stay away!"

Shorty slowly got to his feet. His face was red and sweating. As he turned to walk away, he spat out a plug of whatever he'd been chewing. "I'll get both of you yet," he warned. "Just watch, I'll squeeze you and get that buried treasure out of you."

"Asshole!" yelled Danny. He took the stick he carried out of his makeshift scabbard and threw it on the ground. He whispered to Beth, "I don't need this from him."

Shorty's fist clenched and waved in the air. Inaudible mumbling spewed from his lips.

Beth shook her head. So much for reminiscing about old times.

"Everything will be all right," reassured Danny, glancing toward Beth.

Perhaps she'd overreacted. During her latest trip to the river, she had stuck her finger in the water and the fish had swum away. Just as the fish had adapted to fear, Beth realized she had adapted to fear in her own way. Holding her breath helped stop a flood of tears.

~ * ~

Shorty's tears flowed like water at Niagara Falls. At his camp, he fashioned a strong vine into a hangman's noose. Climbing to the top of a coconut tree, he secured the vine around the trunk. Around his broken leg's foot, he tightened the noose's loop. For over an hour, he hung tightly to the tree and sobbed. Reaching toward the knots, he lost his footing and slipped. While in full flight, he screamed loud enough to be heard across South America.

~ * ~

"Beth," said Danny. Staying in the shade of the crude hut, he paced back and forth. "We need a change of scenery. If you like, you can use the compass and GPS to help map the magnetic northern part of the island."

"Yes!" She leapt off the log. "But it may take time to learn."

He smiled. "We'll find time. In case something happens to me, at least you'll be familiar with your directions." When he strapped on the magnetometer, it covered most of his stomach area. Holding the microphone's staff with one hand, he plugged its cable into the magnetometer with the other. He adjusted the time and magnetic intervals to be recorded every three seconds.

He passed her the GPS. "Each time I wave, press the main button to record the unit's position and time. Some other day, I'll rig up the computer to it. Then, it could record every three seconds like my magnetometer." He handed her a compass. He explained, "I'll turn its face until the red line faces the cross-section's direction. Keep the needle pointing to the north but follow the red line. Lead me in that direction."

"I can do that." Her body tingled in anticipation of starting.

They headed toward a part of the island where Danny left off a couple of days before.

Twenty

Beth took the lead, carrying both the GPS and the compass.

Part ways through the survey, Danny stopped. "Any questions?"

She felt excited that her scientific efforts were appreciated, and that she speeded up the project. Checking it out, she knew she had to ask. "What is this survey about?"

"Diamonds," he explained. "Just try to keep the compass away from the GPS's metal." Using both hands he held a long, plastic staff with a large, magnetic microphone screwed into the top end, high into the air. A magnetometer had been fastened to the front of his body, with straps, at stomach level. He glanced at the sun. "You're doing fine."

"How can you tell?"

"Well," he answered, "I look at the position of the sun and the time. I can tell pretty much the direction we're moving that way."

Being in the lead, she walked slowly. "Is this too fast?"

"You're the one that has to stop for bearings." He smiled. "The reason I keep slowing down is because I have to stay a certain distance away from your GPS's battery pack, and your compass's metal magnetic field. Otherwise, hell, I can run. We both have to move at the same time because the computer is set up to subtract the distance between us. A little bit out is okay."

"We're actually searching for diamonds?" Now that seemed a little far-fetched. "We might even run into more gravesites with this too, huh?"

"Sure could."

Perhaps he was a treasure seeker all along, claiming to be a mineral explorer, she guessed. "How big is a diamond field?"

"Depends," began Danny. "It's the width of a volcano or its parts. Most are usually fifty meters around but can be up to two miles in circumference. Small offshoots or veins can stream away from a main volcanic vent. It they cool fast enough, diamonds can be a by-product. All vents go down miles."

She only owned one diamond and she liked having it very much. Her father had given her the ring for her first teenage birthday. Constant nagging, hinting, and threatening had paid off in order to acquire it. It had been a small diamond, but she recalled that it had looked big when she had flashed the sparkling rock in other girls' faces. Now mountains of diamonds were near to her. "How are diamonds usually found?"

After hesitating, he replied, "Sometimes you get a large bulldozer to scrape a couple of inches at a time and you can walk along behind and pick up the visible diamonds. Trainloads! Then you run the rest of the soil through large separators as you would gold."

"Wow!"

"Sure," he added. "Maybe the whole island is one large diamond field."

"Get real." The thought of a large vent laying billions of diamonds under her feet seemed to change the landscape. Before it was beautiful, breathtaking, and now it was salvation, staggering. The biotite sparkled in the sunlight, inviting her to run over to take a closer look. She restrained herself. "What about all the shinny rock?"

"Most of them are called indicator metallic minerals."

"How far down?"

"They can start only a few feet from the ground."

Taking a large breath, her eyes darted around, searching for outcrops. She could picture herself digging around just about everywhere in her free time. Had that been the reason for the open shallow gravesite? Perhaps Danny wanted to keep his digging secrete. "Did you already start any digging?"

"No," he replied. "Not yet. I like to wait until I have everything mapped out. Then I'll dig around and check for samples."

"I see," she said. It must've had been Shorty with the telling evidence of dead animals nearby. Maybe it wasn't even intended to be a gravesite. There was no sense in upsetting Danny over it though, so she kept quiet. She recalled how weird Shorty acted during his brief visit. "Gold has caused many men to do strange things."

"Beg your pardon?"

"Well," she explained, walking in the direction he indicated. "Sometimes people do strange things for money."

"Let's keep our mind on our jobs," he said curtly. "That's enough bullshit." Apparently he was too busy to talk any more.

She felt small. Had he picked up on what she had said? She looked down at her feet. "I'm sorry."

Narrowing both eyelids and lips, he cast another look of disdain.

They walked in silence.

While her mouth watered with the thought of truckloads of the precious gems, she wondered why she had been so stupid to sour the chance of a share. Being in front of him, she believed he could read into her movements. Unlike a thirsty dog, she knew she better keep her diamond tasting tongue from hanging out in public.

Holding her head up, she focused on her task of staying in one direction. Letting him concentrate on his job, she decided to let him begin their conversations. After work could be another story.

Twenty One

After a couple of months of work, Danny pointed at a computer-generated map on the laptop. "Looks like two large magnetic fields exist on the north side of the island. The rest of the island area has a lot lower readings. The highs look like contour elevations of a couple of mountains and are definite anomalies. Let's go look into them."

They walked at a brisk pace to view them close up.

Beth saw that the first prospect consisted of a mound about fifty feet high, and that it fit perfectly to the contours of the magnetic readings. Many large trees with lots of branches close together stood on the top of the small hill. Did trees like that usually grow on diamond mounds? She didn't ask Danny. Instead, Beth cried gleefully as the many colorful birds sang, and the small hairy monkeys played and jumped on each other.

"Starts here," Danny pointed. "And extends for three hundred meters that way and one hundred and fifty meters both north and south."

"It's the hill," she sighed. "And it's breathtaking."

"It's beaming with life." He shrugged his shoulders. "I'd have to replant the whole thing in another location to keep the life thriving. The animals probably use this area for safety."

"You'd do that?" Beth asked. Her eyes widened at the thought of Danny doing something so special.

"Sure," he said. "I'd like to impact the surroundings as little as possible. With a diamond mine you have the choice to do everything." He started climbing up. "We may as well walk over it. The other one is close to this one."

"Here is the one with the strongest readings." Danny climbed the hump at the second anomaly. "It's circular, about five hundred meters around."

Scrutinizing the area, Beth saw small trees and less wildlife. The noise level of the animals was quieter. A few monkeys inhabited one clump of trees, similar to the other trees on the other hill. Here, the outer trees camouflaged a thicker inner clump of trees.

Standing beside Danny, she studied his movements. His eyes seemed to take in everything at once. When he seemed to be fixed on one area, she found that she had to look away from him to try to see what he saw.

"You can see quite a ways from here," he said. "It's like an optical illusion. Hardly any trees seem to be there but there really are lots. The monkeys seem to accept us here. They are quiet—"

"Maybe they sense our better qualities," she cut in.

With his lips tightened into his mouth, he shot her a look of disgust. "Whatever," he said.

She quieted, wary that he looked on the verge of backhanding her to shut her up. Her brows furrowed. He wasn't so grouchy when they'd first started out today, but he was getting crankier as the day progressed.

In a drowning, harsh voice he continued. "We'll be spending a lot of time here, collecting readings and samples."

"That's a good idea," she blurted excitedly.

He set about moving logs into various positions and sat on one. With his hand, he motioned her to sit on the other.

She gratefully accepted his offer. There had to be

something intelligent; something witty she could say to get him to appreciate her. "Well, if we find diamonds," she started, "even if we have to stay on this island for life, at least we'll be rich."

He leaned forward and laughed.

His laughter was contagious and it wasn't long before she too was laughing.

They joked and called the place *Beth's Bank*. It was good to see Danny relaxed again, even if it were only for a few minutes. Beth didn't much like his grumpy side. She didn't even mind when he wanted to leave some food behind at their makeshift work site for the next day's work.

The next day, they found the food stores missing at Beth's Bank.

"Looks like some animal robbed the bank," commented Danny. Finding a large flat piece of dried, gray wood, he moved sand. "I'm going to dig down to see what minerals I can find."

"I'll help too." She found a long, wide stick and then looked for guidance.

"Dig there." He pointed to a low spot ten feet off to his right.

At noon they stopped and collected a few small samples. They put them beside the test-hole and pushed some sand back into it.

Both sweated profusely in the midday sun. They went to sit in the shade of their small camp's trees. After a half-hour, he climbed a tree and began chatting like a monkey.

Laughing freely, she felt on top of the world. Life looked wonderful. She liked Danny's sense of humor while digging for diamonds.

"Come on up," he dared. "Join in the fun of your ancestors."

Laughing, she leapt off the log she was sitting on. Her strong biceps muscles pulled her easily into the thick branches. High in the tree, she beat her chest. She cried loudly, "Me Jane!"

Smiling, Danny leapt out of the tree onto another.

Squealing with excitement, she clapped her hands high in the air. Closing her eyelids, she sprang about four feet to a nearby tree and hung on. Giggling, she opened them and looked at Danny for feedback.

With his mouth gaping open, he held up his hands as though being taken prisoner. Through a garbled, nervous laugh he cautioned, "Try it again with your eyes open."

She did, realizing an accomplishment, and kept going. At the end of the day she could leap around in the trees well enough. Finding as long as she concentrated on one jump at a time, she could gain quite a bit of ground safely. In her houseboat, Beth slept soundly that night.

~ * ~

The sun peaked over the horizon into the open window of Beth's raft and penetrated her eyelids. Blinking, she could see the clear skies of a new day. It was already warm as she attempted to get out of bed. "Danny!" she cried over to the other raft. "I can't move."

Danny's voice cut into the stillness of the early morning air. "You're super sore," he explained. "You worked new muscles. No pain, no gain. Get your ass into gear and move around a bit to stretch out."

It hurt to stand. She took her first step and almost cried because of the pain. She grimaced and sat back on her bed. "Ouch!"

A few minutes later, she still didn't know what to do. She knew she had to get up. Logic dictated that Danny was right, she had to stretch. Pain dictated otherwise.

"Here," Danny appeared next to her raft with a few fresh pineapples. "Let's get your strength up and get you moving."

She was good as long as she stayed put, and the small, sweet pineapples were a welcome breakfast. Her mind wandered along old paths. She had a condition. That was it. She knew she must break it to Danny. She told him that her condition required medical help, and that she would never be able to leave the raft. Maybe all the varying aches and pains she had described were the truth.

Apparently Danny would have none of her story because well before noon, they jumped for joy and laughed themselves sick while outdoing themselves on the trees.

About a month went by of playing games of camouflage and of tag on the trees. While chinning herself a strong branch, she felt powerful and asked Danny to check out the new, flexed lump on her arm. After he approved, she strutted around comparing herself to Jane. She noticed Danny laughing encouraging along with her.

She had started to shape up and knew it. The proper food and exercises had accomplished wonders beyond belief. She felt super good and her confidence soared.

They began playing a game of tag. With Danny slacking off, she got a big head start. Partially hidden, she laid back in the comfort of some thick branches and teasingly opened her legs. She had been a virgin long enough.

Danny stopped a few feet away and turned away.

"I love you," she groaned. Waving with her hands, she motioned him to come nearer and opened her legs as wide as she could. "I want you to make love to me right here and now!"

Remaining silent, he looked straight at her. Then he moved slowly towards her and started climbing the tree.

"Yes," she called out, closing her eyes. "Mine forever." Her mind reeled at the thought of holding him tightly. She opened her arms. Then, she heard the branches rustle and a thud on the sand.

Before she could think, Danny had dropped out of the tree and headed in the direction of the rafts.

Their relationship came to a grinding halt. He hadn't liked her, like she thought. He'd only wanted to get close to her and to have her drop her guard. Stories in horror magazines came to mind about people like him and gold fever. Sure, that's why he had turned ugly, during the magnetic survey, when she mentioned that money does strange things to people. She pieced together that he likely told her about the diamonds before thinking about it, and that he'd have to get rid of her so he could have it all for himself. Tears of humiliation filled her eyes.

To add insult to injury, a monkey climbed in the tree above her and made laughing noises.

Twenty Two

Smiling for the first time in a long time, Shorty laid on a bed of palm leaves, pleased as punch. Searching for signs of a treasure, he had been spying on Danny and Beth for a long time. Waiting had paid off; now he must play his cards right to take advantage of Beth's frustration.

Recalling her legs spread; how she beckoned a man to come inside her, Shorty moaned. How could Danny just walk away from a piece of ass? When Shorty left a woman, it was usually after having sex rather than before. He could find her sweet spot before Danny ever could. In two shakes, Shorty's hand jerked up and down until the moans climaxed and the slapping ceased.

In the silence that followed, a large rodent scampered into the hut and dragged out a large portion of cooked meat. As the rat got out the doorway, Shorty fired a palm branch after it.

Twenty Three

For the following weeks, Beth spent much of her time at the trees watching the monkeys play. Knowing Danny usually left early to check out the magnetic sites, she had stayed as far away as possible. Not only was she mortified over her behavior and his lack of interest, but also she was again convinced that both Shorty and Danny were planning to do her in. She wasn't going to take it lying down, not in this lifetime. With both men having it in for each other, turning the tables on them should be easy enough.

She got up to wash when she heard Danny stir in the morning. "I think we should make friends with Shorty. He's been by himself for a long time and might go crazy. Who needs that? I'm going over to talk to him."

Danny swallowed a sizeable amount of water and started coughing. "I better go with you."

"No. I'll be safe. He could hardly walk last time we saw him. Besides, he doesn't like you very much." Believing she sounded convincing, she plunged into the water and swam away before he could answer.

When the coughing stopped, he dove in and swam for shore. When he got there, he headed towards Shorty's camp. He stopped himself and sat down. "I hope you know what you're doing."

~ * ~

Beth slowly stepped into the clearing of the camp and immediately cringed. Insects were everywhere. Seeing only a small fire burning where they had set the first signal fire led her to believe it likely burned nights and likely to scare wild animals away. Looking closer into the burn, she saw a wild pig gnawing on some flesh still attached to partly burnt deer antlers. She called, "Shorty."

Fast moving stepping sounded in the sand. Turning in the direction of the rafts, she expected to see Danny. It turned out to be Shorty, or someone resembling him.

He looked like he was dragged through a knothole. Knotted beard and hair covered his sunburned head. His torn clothes were filthy. Her nose crinkled. His stench was overpowering. That one man could stink so badly when one of the largest oceans of the world sat nearby was hard to believe.

Gazing in the direction he came from, she realized that he must've had been spying. At least it was something definite. She felt glad to put an end to his lurking around in the dark waiting to strike. Seeing him walk upright, though, without a limp, sent chills through her spine. "It's Danny," she explained, "He used me as a work horse, and now he wants to do away with me."

Shorty pursed his lips and looked doubtful. He rolled his hand forward, motioning her to continue.

"He'll get you next," she added. "He wants it all for himself."

"Yes, the treasure." His voice had that faraway sound, and his eyes looked vacant. He sat on a nearby log. Pointing at another close by, he gestured her over to sit. "You know where it is?"

"Yes," she admitted, flitting over to the log. Reaching over to brush it off, she flexed her biceps and watched for a response. He didn't seem to notice. Instead, he was busily trying to straighten out his hair. She sat down and waited in silence for him to speak.

"Listen, I know what you want," he stated bluntly. "If you want me to do something, it's going to cost you. Otherwise get the hell out of my camp."

"Yes, of course." She stood up, shaken he could read her so well. Reaching down, she dusted the seat again, hoping he'd think it was why she leapt up. After stretching, she sat back down. "I know where Danny thinks the treasure is. You can have all of it, just do it right away."

"You got yourself a deal." He reached to shake an agreement.

"One thing, you'll have to wait until we're rescued before I tell you," she said, getting louder as she spoke to hide her shakes. "It'll make sure I stay alive. If you try something, I'll lead you to the wrong spot and you'll never see a penny." She extended her hand.

"Okay," he agreed.

"Okay."

His beady eyes darted over his shoulder.

"I'm alone," she said. "Don't worry."

"I'm not worried," he claimed. "How do you want to do it?"

"For one thing, he thinks you're a cripple," she began. "So, act like one. I'll tell him I trust you and want you to come over more often. Of course, you'll have to clean up. We want everything to go smoothly. Then we'll get him to push my raft and prepare it for travel right away. When he drops his guard, you know what to do."

"Is it planned like the previous screw up?"

"This time it'll be different."

"I'm really past being embarrassed."

"I promise."

~ * ~

Danny spent the time waiting for Beth to return by

gathering fruits and vegetables. With the food in a pile, he paced back and forth. Then, he sat down and stared toward the rafts.

Before noon, she showed up on the shore of the lake where he waited. She complimented his work ethic. "What a fine bunch of food you gathered."

He rushed close. "How did it go?"

"He said he'd like to be our friends and make another attempt at mainland. I'd like to go with him."

"So, he thinks he'd be better off on the ocean."

"Yes, he is pretty lonely. He's had enough." With a half smile, Beth said that as though speaking about her as well as Shorty.

"Well, I'll do what I can to help," claimed Danny.

"Thanks."

"I can stock the raft by tonight."

"Thanks."

"Hey. No problem."

"Danny, please watch out. He could try something again."

"Yes, that I will." He dove in the water, swam to the raft, and began pushing it towards the ocean. She helped all she could.

In the late afternoon they had the craft at the mouth of the ocean. Shorty still kept away, and they kept working.

Danny showed Beth how to use the map in relation to the GPS in case something happened to Shorty. Having worked with the unit while mapping the island, she caught on quickly and placed the unit and maps on the raft. Before long, they set about filling the craft with food and water.

She straightened her back and wiped her brow. "Dusk is starting to set in. It may be a good idea to complete the packing to allow for an early start. The largest bunches of coconuts are at the trees where we used to climb."

Danny smiled and attempted a joke. "It'll give you a

chance to say good-bye to your animal friends. They'd have it no other way."

Beth thought he was too relaxed about her leaving the island. He should tread carefully because she knew about the diamonds. She took a deep breath, hoping that Shorty would make his entrance soon. They headed towards the large magnetic anomaly, with her leading the way.

~ * ~

While picking the coconuts needed for the trip, she found a sharp stick and put it in her cache of nuts. Knowing Shorty would be appearing soon, she had to prepare for him as well as Danny and then take her chances on the ocean. If this was the last she'd see of Danny, she wanted to know why he hated her so. Bluntly, she asked, "Why do you dislike me?"

"I...I like you," he stammered. "It's your resemblance to my ex-wife that bothers me."

She felt like puking. Everything seemed to click a different way. Maybe, it was a case of her own ego rather then Danny hating her. She could completely understand disliking being around someone who resembled someone you hated. Cripes, she couldn't stand her ex, and if she were stuck on a deserted island with him or someone who looked and acted like him, she'd have a hard time of it too.

A rustling nearby caught her attention. It was Shorty sneaking up on Danny. What had she done? She dropped her coconuts.

Danny knelt to pick them up.

Shorty leapt. A hardwood staff raised high.

"Holy shit!" Beth cried out.

Shorty paused for a brief moment and glared at her before continuing the swing.

Danny moved to the side, pushing out his arm in defense. The stick glanced off his shoulder.

The momentum threw Shorty off balance, and he fell

backward onto the white sand and some sharp pieces of black biotite.

Grabbing a coconut with his good arm, Danny pitched it at Shorty. It bounced off his head, knocking him out. Rubbing where the blow hit, Danny got up and turned toward Beth.

In one motion, she knelt down, picked up the stick, and sprang on Danny. Forcing him on his back, the sharp stick pressed slightly into his throat. She gulped. No matter how much she tried, she couldn't bring herself to press harder. His hand gripped and turned her wrist. The pain grew with every passing second and if she didn't stop him soon, she'd suffer a broken wrist. As she let the weapon loose, she rolled in the direction of the twist to prevent the bones from breaking. Once beside Danny, she felt him release her and watched him stand up.

"Stay away from me!" he shouted angrily. He waved the sharp stick over both of them. "I've had all I can take. Both of you better stay away from me!"

Beth turned on her stomach.

"Yeah you'd better be ashamed of yourself."

Danny wasn't moved by her sobs. Not this time. "I'm sorry," she apologized. "Please forgive me."

"Me too." responded Shorty, still dazed. "She talked me into it."

"I believe it," admitted Danny. He grabbed Shorty's ankle with one hand and placed his other arm higher under the leg. He dropped down with his knee, causing Shorty's tibia bone to snap. Then, Danny got back to his feet. "Do it again, and I'll break something higher than your shinbone. Understand?"

"Yes!" Shorty pleaded. He turned pale with pain. "Please leave me alone."

"Keep the GPS you got." After kicking sand on them, Danny walked away. "The sooner you leave the better. Good riddance."

Beth followed Shorty into his rundown shack. Animal remnants and leftover food littered everywhere. Flies appeared willing to share the plentiful bounty with other insects. A health inspection came to mind, but understanding the mind-boggling events of the day became a priority. Since the attempted bushwhacking, Beth remained quiet. She'd never seen a man cry before, so she knew Shorty was in extreme pain. She stopped walking and waited to be told what she should do next.

Shorty sat on a stump close to the door, stretching out his broken leg. After putting the stick he used as a crutch on the floor next to him, he stared at Beth through red, teary eyes.

Breaking the silence, she spoke softly. "The best-laid plans of mice and men go off astray."

"Is that some kind of Shakespeare?" He looked ready to spring out of his chair and beat her.

"I don't know," she answered in a whisper.

"When my leg gets better," fumed Shorty, "I'll murder that zipper-head." Sneering at her, he touched on plan B, "This time I'll do it myself. He'll never know what hit him. Killing is the only way to handle things."

"Yes, the only way," she agreed. She tried to sound convincing, but deep down she believed his words to be a threat to her too. Out on the ocean, he had tried leaving her for dead for less. She remembered his fingers tugging at her laces forcing her to relinquish her lifejacket. She shuddered and tried to block out the memories. Without a doubt, she realized her warnings to Danny hardly put her in Shorty's good book. Shorty's new threats appeared out of his element as long as he sported the broken leg, even to her.

"You sleep there," he said, pointing to the back end of the hut. "I'll sleep here by the door and openings in case Danny or a wild animal tries to get in while we sleep."

Knowing his explanation was open to question, because Danny could've had finished them off earlier, put her on edge. Instead of making trouble by arguing, she slunk to the enclosed part of the hut and sat down in the darkness on the leaves. Palm leaves had been stacked up, making an extra bed. She wondered when Shorty had prepared a spare mattress for her but knew better than to ask. Besides, after all the work she had done earlier, she welcomed the rest on a soft bed.

"Can I get you something?" he asked.

"No thanks," she uttered through a clogged throat.

"Water or food?" he pushed.

"No," she said. It sounded like a whine, but she decided to leave it at that. She didn't want to owe him anything. Everything seemed out of place. Throughout most of the night, she whimpered and cried. At two in the morning, she dropped off.

Out of nowhere, his six foot five inch frame leapt on her. The weight of his strong muscles held her in place. Limiting her movement, his right hand gripped her left wrist and pushed it high over her head. "Now you're in for it!"

Unsure of what was going on, she squirmed. Half asleep, she kicked and punched at anything her fist or foot connected with. Her mouth closed down on the dirty skin of Shorty's left hand.

He pulled his hand free and walloped the side of her head with a closed fist.

Spitting out blood and skin, she turned her head into her armpit for protection.

He undid his pants and shoved his elbow between her legs to pry them apart.

Rape! He was trying to rape her? The hell with that! She interlocked her feet and kept her legs together. How could she be so stupid as to forget to stash a weapon close by? Shorty was scum. She shouldn't have let him surprise her like this.

"Get off me!" she panted and struggled beneath his bigger bulk.

"Be still!" he warned. His open hand cuffed her face.

Transferring the pain, she bit down on her lip until it bled. She reached out to hit his broken leg but his kneecap was too far away. Defeating him might not be possible.

He pushed against her and tried forcing his penis between her locked thighs but she held on, refusing to allow him entry.

After a few pumps at the space between her legs, he climaxed and rolled away. Through heavy gasps for air, he uttered, "I'm sorry. Please forgive me."

She leapt up, tugging her dress down over her hips. "Fuck off!" Blood sprinkled out of her cut mouth as she spoke. "You should have died on that raft, you don't deserve to breathe. You're nothing but a creep!"

Rolling away, he remained silent.

She gave him a kick and sprinted out of the doorway. What the hell had happened to start all of this shit tonight? Right! Her planning the murder of two people probably had something to do with it. Well, she wouldn't do that again. She'd had enough excitement to last a lifetime tonight.

"Come back!" Shorty called after her. "You can't hide! You're all mine."

Heading for safety, she raced her tears. The harder she cried, the faster she ran.

~ * ~

In the morning, Danny walked by the large magnetic anomaly to the trees. A red-eyed, tear-stained Beth huddled in the branches of one.

"What's wrong?" He bent down and took another look. "Can I come closer?"

She began to sob.

"I hoped you'd be here," claimed Danny. "I'm glad you're all right. I forgive you for jumping on me. I realize you're under a lot of stress. We both came a long way from the beginning. I must've put you in a bad mood to change you."

"He tried raping me," she blurted out. She raised red-rimmed eyes to his face.

Danny moved closer, but still kept his distance.

"He hit me." Pointing to the side of her face, she closed her eyes and felt the tears hang in her eyelashes. "Here, and here and here." Wherever she experienced pain, she highlighted the spot with her finger.

"Jeez!" His fists clenched. "You're all black and blue."

She wiped at the blood around her mouth. She held her chin high. "It's not so bad, really." Her lips trembled. She was putting on a brave face for him. She must trust Danny a little bit to come back to him after the experience with Shorty.

"This is the last straw!" Smacking his fist into the palm of his other hand, he pressed his lips tightly together. "If it's the last thing I do, I'm going to finish off that bastard." Danny got to his feet and left in the direction of Shorty's camp.

~ * ~

She climbed out of the tree and lay on the warm sand beneath it. After sleeping a couple of hours, Danny's approaching footsteps woke her.

"He's left the island," he said. "I've searched all over. The raft is gone.'

"Danny," she started. "You don't you like me, do you?"

"I like you," he said. "I really do. Unlike what I experienced with my ex-wife, you are really turning out more beautiful as each day passes."

"I feel so bad," she sobbed. "I like you too. I don't know why it happened. I've betrayed you. Can you believe it, betrayal in paradise?"

"Mistakes can happen." Moving slowly, he sat down and looked at her. "It's not only you."

"Thank you," she squeaked her response and looked up into his eyes. "I don't know what to do." Patting the ground beside her, she urged him to sit.

Instead, he kneeled. "Do you realize if we hugged, it'd be the first time?"

Reaching up, she claimed, "This one time would make up for everything."

After the hug, he stretched out on the sand beside her and held her head in his arm. "You've been through a lot."

Lying still, she thought any movement might change things. Saying nothing, she closed her eyes. When he touched her hair, she could feel the bad memories being pulled from her. She never knew each hair had its own nerve. As she drifted off, the next thing Danny said sounded like a dream.

"You've been through more than any woman I've ever known."

In a couple of hours she woke up, reached over and put her hand on the back of his head.

While gingerly touching her face with his free hand, he pushed ahead until their lips met.

"Make love to me," she moaned

He pulled the dress slowly from her body while she beckoned him closer. "Please, just don't stop."

After hesitating, he undressed.

"I love you." Through her closed eyes, the vision of him getting closer played in her brain. She squeezed her eyelids tight. "I need you more then ever!"

"Beth," asked Danny. "Are you sure?"

Before she could answer, she felt his skin on hers and when he finally groaned, she lost control of her own body and spiraled upward to the heavens.

The animals ran around in circles, screaming at the top of their lungs. The fish swam swiftly in all sorts of directions. Birds filled the sky, creating a strobe effect with their shade. Beth realized all that, and more.

Twenty Four

To Danny, the picturesque island seemed to beam of love, health, and togetherness. Now with the Midas' ears lifted from him, he learned to appreciate the love of a woman. Even the corn kernels Beth had planted when they first arrived took hold and developed into a small crop. Danny noticed how well animals adjusted to her, and how well she adjusted to them. Occasionally, when birds landed on Beth's outstretched hand, they ate the kernels and the seeds she offered. Some animals seemed to go out of their way to cross right in front of her to see what she would do. Either she stopped to let them pass, or she spent hours talking softly as though they understood. It made Danny happy to see her happy.

They mapped the magnetic fields of the southern half of the island in four months. This had taken so long because Shorty had taken the GPS. Instead, Danny had Beth lay out landmarks and marked the time of each reading at each landmark. Once the drift of the mobile magnetometer was subtracted from the drift of the stationary magnetometer, he fed the time of each reading at each landmark into the small laptop. Now, he had a professional idea of the highs and lows. Before deciding to make smaller grids, he and Beth set out digging promising rock and soil samples.

By the thickly netted trees, he ran magnetic tests every twenty feet. In the heart of an anomaly with high readings, he discovered a super high magnetic channel about twenty five feet wide and one hundred and fifty feet long.

"A fissure super cooled in the vent faster through here," pointed out Danny. "It must've cooled, cracked, and super cooled. Whatever the case, it looks promising."

"Do you think—?"

"We'll dig down and find out," cut in Danny. Pulling the sides of his lips back as tight as he could, he smiled his pearly whites.

With arms waving high, she leapt high into the sky. "At last I get to see diamonds."

He held up his hand. "We still have lots of work to do."

Believing the task to be big, they spent a full day carving various sizes of shovels and pickaxes. Getting an early start the next day, they took some time and stared quietly at the blessing in appreciation before starting any clearing.

Twenty Five

Digging into the sand, Beth found she loved work more and more as time passed. Danny was a difficult taskmaster, but all the hard work and strict discipline paid off. She was with him when he discovered a couple of possible buried treasure tombs, a couple of probable bottomless diamonds' vents, and now a highly likely diamond fissure channel. With her luck, maybe the colour of the diamonds varied in each area. Throughout the day it had been all business, but at nights, she enjoyed the pleasure of passionate lovemaking.

After a week's digging, they barely made a dent. They cleared an area twenty feet wide by twenty-five feet long by seven feet deep. They needed a break, and decided to take a couple of days off and rest their calluses.

~ * ~

Beth's goal was to remove all traces of Shorty's existence on the island. She liked the idea of burning the shack and anything else that reminded them of him. While old animal skins could come in handy for blankets and clothing, it just looked bad to the friendly animals on the island. Danny agreed to help her clean and burn the area.

They built a fire over Shorty's latrine area. There were so many odd looking bugs and insects that the only explanation could be that they came for the undigested meat and the droppings of a meat eater. It made her notice that her sweat never stank. She kept the fires blazing all through the first day.

On the second day, they gathered what was left in the ashes. The unburned logs and such would burn for a second time at the signal fire.

Danny mixed the ashes into the sand, using a flat piece of wood. "The area looks more natural now."

"It looks like we removed the last of the bad memories," agreed Beth. "Good riddance to bad rubbish."

"You got it." He motioned Beth to sit down and then stopped short. He tilted his head toward the humming sound that seemed to get louder. Before he could say another word, he pointed out a powerboat racing into the cove toward the remaining drifts of smoke.

At first Beth was elated. Rescued at last! But would it be the end of her newfound happiness? Parting with Danny would hurt. He'd probably go back to his life, and she'd have to go back to hers. After all, diamond mining was a big operation. Even if he cut her in, it was unlikely the owners worked in the area of the mining. Oh well, it was fun while it lasted and she even got in shape. Like the best spa treatment ever. She got to her feet and slowly moved to greet her rescuer.

He was clean-cut. Wearing a large black cowboy hat and dark sunglasses, the man steered the diesel powered boat their way. Both his hands remained on the wheels until he got to within about thirty feet of shore. After cutting the throttle, he used the other hand to reach deep into the interior. When the boat glided on to the sandy shore, the man jumped over the side sporting a rifle.

Twenty Six

Beth watched in horror as Danny stopped, turned, and sprinted, closing gap between him and her. At the crack of the rifle, she cringed while his right shoulder exploded with blood, flesh, and bone spurting everywhere. He dropped in full flight.

With her mind reeling, she raced back to the safety of some trees. Gasping for breath, she chanced a peak and saw Danny lying still. This couldn't be happening.

The shooter skirted past him at a dead run. Beth had to hide. She had to get to the thick covering of the trees near the large magnetic anomaly.

The shooter glanced at the blood stained body on the ground. Without slowing, he headed in Beth's direction. Even when he lost sight of her, he checked places she had only gone to when alone. Without a doubt, Shorty's days of spying had paid off.

Beth hid quietly under a tree's large branches. As each second ticked by, she heard the birds and the monkeys get louder and louder. She breathed deeply to calm her shivering body. Who the hell had shot the gun? There was no rhyme or reason for it. The sounds around her stilled and she sensed he was close. Cold steel touched her shoulder as the barrel of the .223 caliber rifle found its mark. She stiffened as a wave of nausea threatened to bring up her lunch.

"Get up!" commanded the voice. "Thought you could hide, huh? I know you better than you know yourself."

Recognizing the voice, she understood why he needed her alive. Slowly, she got to her feet.

"Double-crossing bitch!" he sneered. "You thought that you could have it all to yourself."

He was mad, truly mad. Shorty's beady eyes moved quickly around in their sockets. "You're walking?"

"Unreal what a few months can do under a doctor's care, huh?"

"Why are you back?" She asked the question, not really wanting to hear the answer.

"You know why I came back!"

At the ugly tone in his voice, her bladder let go. He was going to kill her. She had faced so many dangers and survived, but she didn't think she could survive this one. He had already killed Danny. Having little to lose, she acted as brave as possible. Fluttering her eyelids, she acted as if she felt flattered he thought of her. "You came for me?"

"Ha!" He retorted. "Yes, for me! Yes! You're right!" He laughed, but stopped and lowered his voice. "Don't try and piss me off."

"Oh?" She played stupid. "I know as little as you do about any treasure. I told you I did so you'd help me out."

"Right, I almost fell in its large hole," he said sarcastically. He pointed in the direction of the anomaly. "So that's where it was buried."

"What do you mean?"

His fist met her teeth. Her head spun back, but she remained upright.

"So, what did you do with it?"

"Do with what?"

Opening his hand, he cuffed the side of her face. This time she spit a bit of blood and a piece of tooth out.

Holding the tears back, she covered her face with her hands for protection.

Lifting his hand high, he prepared to strike again.

"No," she cried. "We're still digging for it. That's why the tools are still there."

Pointing with his rifle, he motioned her to go in the direction of the freshly dug hole. Following her, he strapped the rifle to his back. Moving slowly, she reasoned he could kill her without the gun at the drop of a hat.

Picking up the pace, his large paw pushed her forward. "Move it."

At the hole, he ordered, "Dig!" When she slowed down, he threatened, "Move faster!"

She worked hard, knowing he had little reason to keep her alive.

After removing the bullet clip, he ejected the bullet out of the chamber and set the rifle on the bank made by the excess sand. Grasping one of the makeshift shovels, he shoveled and probed in the sandy bottom. When the wood banged against something solid, he concentrated on clearing it. After finding rock after rock, he complained, "You call these tools?"

Remaining silent, she kept busy in the dig. Soon the night closed in.

"All this friggin green rock is slowing us down." He hurled a large chunk of diamond bearing kimberlite at her. "It seems to be all there is."

She jumped over her wooden scoop to avoid the missile. She grimaced in pain as the rock scraped the skin on her upper arm. Keeping busy, she positioned herself as far away as possible from him.

Climbing out of the hole, he picked a bunch of apples off a nearby tree. Without explanation, he threw one hard near her feet.

This was crazy. She stopped work and stood still. It

would be a matter of time before he realized it was a wild goose chase. How would he take being jacked around? If he executed her swiftly, the secrets of the gravesites and diamond would go with her. If slowly, she'd likely tell all. She hoped for a quick end.

"Eat and rest," he ordered, looking tired. "Then get back to work."

He sounded ready to pack it in so she took her time eating the fruit and tried to control her shaking.

"Too bad about Daniel," said Shorty. Tossing the apples ahead, he climbed back into the large hole. "A murder charge is unacceptable."

"No one asked you to kill him."

"He shouldn't have tried to run."

She wanted to tell him that it was wrong, and that it was sick. But instead of flaring Shorty's short temper, she bowed her head and sobbed.

He grabbed her hair and tilted her head upright. While his free hand touched her groin, moving roughly into her softer folds, he spoke close to her ear. "All this could've been yours. Yours and mine, but you ran to him for protection. You left me, as if I was a leper, when I could hardly walk."

"That feels good," she lied. She'd say anything if it meant remaining alive. Saying was one thing though. She couldn't live the reality. His hands on her body made her sick. She turned her head and vomited.

Releasing her, he pushed her away. "What the hell?"

Her face contorted in pain as she bit her swollen lip. Blood poured down her chin. She needed to concentrate on something else to calm her stomach. "The apple was green."

"Perhaps I should drag you to my cabin. We could complete where we left off back there, huh?"

The thought turned her stomach, and she wanted to throw up again. "It's gone," she replied. Talking helped calm her queasiness. "We burned it down as a signal fire."

"Burned all traces of Shorty, huh?" One of his hands reached over and grabbed her hair. He craned her head in the direction of his old encampment. "You thought I was dead and was celebrating! Lost at sea, huh?" His other hand squeezed her throat.

Searching for an answer, her eyes poured out salty, stinging tears. Stars flashed in her eyes, and blackness threatened to envelop her, and then suddenly the grip on her neck slackened.

"Hold it!" commanded Danny. "Let her go." Standing to their back, he held Shorty's rifle in his good arm.

Shorty pushed her away and turned to face Danny, leaving Beth to catch her breath. Once she was able to breathe and some semblance of strength returned to her legs, she clawed her way over the wall to flee as far away as possible.

She stopped, horrified at her next thought. The rifle was empty. He'd probably crawled all evening, weak and hurt, to reach them. He left her little choice but to run for the hills.

"I got the clip right here." Shorty held the clip his hand and waved it in front of Danny.

"You forgot to unload it."

Shorty guffawed. "You're a poor bluffer." Quickly he scaled the bank and yanked the rifle free. He pushed Danny into the hole and scrambled after Beth.

Twenty Seven

Beth raced to the powerboat. It seemed to be the best place to go. After all the time she had spent secluded on the island, she saw the craft as something made by someone intelligent. It contrasted with Shorty, and she felt safer. Safe, until movement caught her eye.

Packing his rifle, Shorty appeared in the clearing.

Doubting he'd shoot up the boat, she searched everywhere for a key. Finding nothing, she tried to push the motorboat into the water.

He was closing in on her fast. Stopping a few feet from her, he laughed insanely and leapt up and down.

He reminded her of a laughing hyena. He was crazy and she didn't have much choice but to run into the water. Swimming hard, she caught a glimpse of him working the vessel into the ocean.

After freeing the powerboat, he pulled the keys out of his pocket and started the motor. With the powerful engine, he caught up to her easily. Remaining seated, he leaned over the side and pushed her head under. His open fingers intertwined with her hair. After almost a minute, he released her.

Surfacing, she gasped for air. Hearing his laughter, she closed her eyes and pushed against the boat with her feet. She swam further out to sea. Her swimming experience allowed her to move swiftly through the water. Saltwater was easier to swim in than the clear lake water, so maybe she had an edge he was unaware of. She headed out into open water.

He roared with laughter, like a rabid madman torturing a turtle. The craft idled behind her, chasing her further out to sea. When she slowed down, he let the bow of the motorboat nudge her onward.

Glancing toward shore, she hoped Danny somehow crawled to the gulf to swim out and save her. Even if he did, she knew he would be little help with one arm. Pressing on, she concentrated on the task at hand. As strong muscles got a second wind, she started to dodge the front of the vessel.

With his rifle strapped to his back, he appeared more serious now and pulled alongside her. After a few attempts to reach her, he got into a kneeling position and extended his reach.

A dolphin appeared between Shorty and Beth and made those funny sounds from so long ago. Shorty was not amused and after rearing back into the motorboat, he freed his gun and fired a few shots at the intruder.

Treading water, Beth saw a part of the fin chip away. Blood darkened the water, giving Beth opportunity to dive and hide. Glancing up at Shorty, she saw him lean over the powerboat to keep an eye on her underwater movements. Another dolphin swam between them through the bloodstained water of the injured mammal.

While taking aim, Shorty jerked and stumbled forward into the water.

Beth swam under him to the other side of the craft and climbed in. She guessed the second dolphin must've had swum around and rammed the motorboat. Smart creatures! Whatever the case, she decided to move the vessel away to a safe distance from Shorty. Her curiosity got the better of her though, and she stopped to watch what happened next.

Instead of playing around, the pissed-off dolphins

pushed him further out to sea. In the distance, Beth saw that his right hand held the .223 high and dry, while the rest of him bobbed up and down. She estimated they moved him along at about twenty-five miles per hour.

"Good for you," remarked Beth out loud to herself. "Have fun in the shark infested waters."

She heard the report of one rifle shot and then he seemed to disappear. Worried about Danny, she headed for shore.

She found him leaning back on the side of the dugout, holding a sharp rock and barely conscious. He kept mumbling something about a rock sample.

"Shush, you have to remain calm. We have to slow the bleeding." Tearing most of her dress and his entire shirt into strips with the sharp rock, she wrapped him the best that she could. She looked into his pain-glazed eyes. "I'm going back for the boat."

Finding the GPS in the powerboat, she reversed the direction of the two readings. When the direction finder pointed in the obvious direction of the mainland, she knew it had been set for the island from the mainland. Seeing the fuel reading in the fuel gauge, she hurried without hesitation.

After about forty miles, Beth spied a boat and headed toward it. Seeing long poles and hanging nets, she assumed it was a fishing boat. A sailor noticed her and pointed at her. Soon, most of its crew lined the safety railings. The sailors jeered and cheered at her near nakedness, but she cared less. Trying to get them to stop the fishing vessel, she waved back by crossing her hands back and forth in front of her. They answered her with lots of whistling followed by Spanish dirty taunts.

When it seemed like they weren't going to stop, she began crashing her motorboat into the side of the larger craft.

Within moments, their horn sounded and they slowed. A rope latter dropped over the side.

Pulling over, she scaled up it in seconds. A couple of fishermen reached down to pull her up. "Captain!" she shouted, "Captain! Please, help!"

Someone pointed to a little control room, housed on the highest part of the vessel.

Almost nude, she ran directly to it. "I need a radio. It's an emergency!' She asked, "Anyone speak English?"

"I speak it." The captain picked up a microphone. "Search and Rescue, come in please."

Off of the GPS hanging from her neck, she read the coordinates to Search and Rescue. Someone threw a blanket over her. Staying put, she guided a helicopter's team to Danny's location. When she mentioned the wounded dolphin, they told her they'd do what they could.

Only after they rescued Danny, she realized what she had been through. In the safety of the ship, she sat down and cried. Only a hurricane could've stopped the continuous flow of tears.

Twenty Eight

Sitting in a six by ten foot whitewashed room, Danny peered through the barred windows at clouds moving in. Thinking about the lazy life his fat wife lived, he realized it would take something like a hurricane to change her. Too bad, he thought, look how Beth turned out.

What had happened to her? The last thing he recalled was her standing over him applying bandages and saying something. Trying to recall what she said, he hoped she made it away from Shorty. Had something horrible happened to Beth or to Shorty, and whom were they blaming for it? Wanting a statement about his bullet wound, the police had kept him in the dark about everything else. He told them that he wanted to wait until his arm healed a bit more. After all, Shorty had carried the rifle and had the odds were on his side. Danny also remembered putting his own fingerprints on the rifle. Every chance he got, he asked for information. No one told him anything.

It was such a long story so he wanted to piece together facts before spending time reliving them. He recalled everything clearly up to a day ago, but he feared that day was the day they were interested in. To top it off, he wondered if his side of the story sounded believable.

Opening his locked door, a prison guard escorted a doctor into his prison cell. While checking out the bandages, the doctor deviated off the topic of the injury. "The dolphin made it okay."

Danny quirked his brows. Okay, the dolphin was good. He guessed that was a good thing as far as dolphins go. He hoped the doctor would sum it up for him and nodded acknowledgement. The doctor appeared to be unaware of the orders to keep him out of the picture.

"No sign of the other fellow's body," he continued.

Hoping he thought he knew what that meant, he cheered inside so loud that his kidney rubbed against his heart. For the first time in days he felt good. He had to know. "Doctor, the woman—"

It didn't take long for a response. "Let me see him," she cried, cutting off Danny's question. "I must see him!"

"Beth!" cried Danny. "I can hear you. I'm okay." Moving toward Beth's voice, he tried pushing the guard aside.

Pushing Danny back, the guard closed the steel door. Then, the guard ran towards Beth. He got to her too late. She made it into the hallway in front of Danny's cell.

"They wouldn't let me see you," she cried.

The guard attempted to push her back out.

"Stop it," ordered the doctor. "You're hurting her."

Danny beat his fists on the door. "Let me out," he shouted. "I want to talk to you too."

"Hold your horses," The guard held his hands over his own ears. "I guess I can allow you to talk separated by the closed door."

"Thank you," Turning to the doctor, Danny asked politely, "First, is the arm going to be all right? I'm sure grateful for all you've done."

"The arm will heal."

"Here's the long and short of it." Before talking to Beth, Danny explained the unusual behavior to the doctor. "They tried to keep me in the dark about what happened to

Beth and Shorty without keeping you posted. Thanks for letting me know about Shorty. Thanks, again, for your help."

While the doctor examined him, Beth told Danny the whole story.

"Beth," he said. "The green rock we had used to cut the strips was kimberlite and diamond. We're rich! Will you marry me?"

Her face fell. "You can keep all of it. You don't have to marry me to get my share. In fact, you can have it all."

"You know I can have just about any woman in the world."

"Likely," she agreed.

"But I want you. I love you." The silence seemed to last forever, but he knew she wouldn't ask him to repeat himself louder.

"Yes," she sobbed.

"Ah Bethie, you'll make a fine wife," he added. "Please, call them in so I could give my statement."

Prologue

After filing a metallic mineral claim on the island, in Peru, South America, Danny used a diamond bearing kimberlite sample to raise enough money to purchase the island. The deal went through because the diamond mine itself would take up the whole island, anyway.

Keeping the wildlife cycle going, Beth and Danny narrowed the mining area and made the rest of the island off limits to everyone. They enjoyed visiting; however, one night, they concluded why others stuck to the mining areas. Beth swore to Danny that she had heard secret digging and unknown footsteps in the night shadows. Was someone searching for the hidden tombs and their hidden treasures? Perhaps it was Shorty, still searching quietly, even in death, for the treasure.

About Danny

Danny Hangartner is a new author with one published novel to his credit. Having searched for diamonds and gravel, he chooses to share some of the geophysical knowledge gained with readers, while keeping them entertained with gritty, entertaining stories.

Also a truck driver, his job is to prove that a tractor-trailer operator is a gentleman of the highway. Danny grew up in Northern Alberta and still resides in Whitecourt, Alberta, where his hobbies continue to be writing and prospecting.

Visit our website for our growing catalogue of quality books.
www.champagnebooks.com

High Risk
by
Jane Toombs

ISBN: 189726139X

Three women flee through mountains that took their friend's life earlier. Now a violent storm rages while a deadly killer trails them...

Send cheque or money order for $16.95 USD
+$4.00 S & H ($20.95) to:
Champagne Books
#35069-4604 37 St SW
Calgary, AB Canada T3E 7C7

Name:	
Address:	
City/State:	ZIP:
Country:	

**From award winning author,
Lori Derby Bingley**

ISBN 1897261497

*One Man. Six Women. And a
Fraternity filled with brothers
who will do anything to keep
their secrets.*

Send cheque or money order for $9.95 USD

+$3.00 S & H ($12.95) to:
Champagne Books

#35069-4604 37 St SW

Calgary, AB Canada T3E 7C7

Name:	
Address:	
City/State:	ZIP:
Country:	

Printed in the United States
74863LV00001B/28-135